Murder in San Felice

Murder in San Felice

Chandralekha Mehta

zubaan

ZUBAAN
an imprint of Kali for Women
128b Shahpur Jat, 1st floor
New Delhi 110 049
Email: zubaan@gmail.com
Website: www.zubaanbooks.com

First published by Zubaan, 2011

10 9 8 7 6 5 4 3 2 1

ISBN: 978 81 89884 85 7

Typeset by Jojy Philip, New Delhi, 110 015
Printed at Raj Press, R-3 Inderpuri, New Delhi 110 012

About the Author

CHANDRALEKHA MEHTA and her sisters grew up in Allahabad where her uncle, Jawarharlal Nehru, and parents were at the very core of the Indian national struggle for independence from British rule. While still in her teens, she was arrested during the Quit India Movement and interned without trial. She worked for the *National Herald*. After her marriage to a diplomat, Ashok Mehta, she lived in a number of countries and continued writing for newspapers and journals. Her earlier book is *Freedom's Child: Growing up during Satyagraha*. This is her first novel.

This is a work of fiction set in the 1970s in San Felice, the capital of a fictitious country somewhere in Latin America. All the characters and incidents are products of the author's imagination and any resemblance to real people and actual incidents is purely coincidental.

Murder in San Felice is a salute to the lands where I spent much of my life as a diplomat's wife. This fantasy of diplomats and murders is dedicated to friendship among people.

ONE

Death of a Count

The news of the murder of Count Jorge de la Bolla reached some citizens of San Felice while they were sipping their morning coffee. Later in the day, the coverage of the newspapers, radio and TV would outrage the local population and cause endless speculation; but this morning, news of the dastardly crime travelled through the grapevine which exists everywhere.

Partaking of his frugal breakfast of coffee and a slice of papaya, the Indian Ambassador learnt of it from his butler Ram Nath, who informed him in suitably solemn tones that Jorge Sahib had been stabbed to death in the night. The shocking news had been communicated to the Ambassador's staff before dawn. A hysterical underling in the Count's home had run sobbing to her sister, Conchita, who was the maid of Shri Bhagwan Narain, Counsellor of the Indian Embassy. The young woman had risked the displeasure of her employers by rushing over to the Embassy residence to tell Gulati Singh, the Embassy cook, with whom she had a tender friendship. Violent death is a sordid event on any occasion, but Count Jorge was a fabulously wealthy, devastatingly good-looking socialite whose every whim and fancy made international jet-setter news. The very fact that crime could dare to touch him, let alone take his life, was incredible. Conchita had had the jitters early in the morning and had to be revived with copious amounts of the Ambassador's best quality Darjeeling tea liberally laced with dollops of cooking sherry.

The Ambassador received the shocking news of his friend Jorge's terrible end with his usual aplomb. It was not in his nature to get excited about anything, and he dismissed Ram Nath with a wave of the hand. He was naturally quite astonished but, as he continued to eat his papaya, he decided that the whole thing could well be a bit of servants' exaggeration. The night before, he had attended one of Jorge's splendid do's and his wife and daughter were still sleeping it off. He had been in great form and, as always, a wonderful host. It was quite possible there had been an attempted burglary, but as for Jorge being stabbed to death – nonsense!

A lean, middle-aged man, the Ambassador was neither short nor tall and had a very ordinary face with thick black hair which was just beginning to grey. His best features were his eyes, which had a contemplative look. He was quiet by nature and gave the impression of possessing great reserves of depth. It was his habit to look steadily with those fine eyes (in his youth, women had sometimes called them bedroom eyes) and listen, rather than take part in conversations. This was because he could not be bothered to make the effort to talk, but it resulted in the general assumption that he was an intellectual and a shrewd diplomat. For years his life had been regulated to an uneventful but pleasant pattern by his wife as well as the exigencies of service; few of his friends realized that beneath his tranquil exterior he was a bubbling cauldron of frustration, longing for another lifestyle and possessions he could not attain. He loved antique French furniture, daggers and the smooth touch of porcelain and he craved to own them all.

But his wife was against the accumulation of what she called junk. "Where will we put that rubbish when we get home?" she would ask, if he broached the subject of satisfying his cravings.

"If you want to buy something, get a good camera or some gadget we don't have at home like an electric toothbrush. And of course we should send for chiffon saris from Hong Kong for Mona's trousseau. What is this nonsense about furniture and china?" Argument was not his forte, especially where his wife was concerned, and in the end the only collection he had been able to manage was a considerable dagger collection. These were his pride and joy. He had found them in markets and second-hand stores in various parts of the world and they were displayed on the wall of his study. The study was his private domain and women rarely entered it; for him it was like an Englishman's club, a refuge from the stress of family life. Sipping his second cup of coffee, he turned his thoughts from domestic matters to work awaiting him in office. Putting down his cup, he neatly folded his table napkin and returned it to the Kashmiri papiêr maché ring in which it was kept. Then he rose and left for the Chancery.

Not far from the Ambassador's residence, in a small villa belonging to the Narains, the mistress of the house was venting her wrath on a sulky, hiccupping Conchita. The breakfast table had not been laid, nor had the kettle been put on for tea and Conchita, at her most slovenly, was not making the least effort to control her tears. As a rule Sheela Narain was not an early riser – certainly not if she had been dancing all night. But this morning she had a long-scheduled dental check-up and, what with the terror inspired by dentists and now Conchita's behaviour, she was close to a tantrum. An attractive woman, she dressed with style and was always well groomed. But not this morning. After hardly any sleep she had wrapped her sari around hastily and not bothered much with make-up. She stamped out of the kitchen where she had been scolding Conchita and saw her husband enter the dining room.

"Any chance of breakfast?" asked Bhagwan, seeing the table bare. "Just a cup of tea will do. I have to rush to office – it's bag day you know." Bag day was the weekly day of preparation to send the diplomatic valise to Delhi; a bustling day of activity in the Chancery, the office of the Indian embassy.

The Counsellor was in his shirt sleeves, his coat and tie over his arm. He looked tired. The previous night had been ruined by a dull and pointless party. He had snatched barely a couple of hours of sleep and had subsequently cut his chin shaving in the morning. He hated these functions and only went because they were either an official duty or, like last night, a social duty impossible to avoid. Playboy parties with champagne and dancing were not to his liking. He loathed both and would have returned home immediately after the buffet except that Sheela, as usual, was nowhere to be seen. Finally he had caught a glimpse of her in the middle of the crowded dance floor, flirting outrageously with some man he did not recognize and then dancing one dance after another with their host.

Sheela was tall and graceful. Last night in her richly brocaded sari, and jewellery from Jaipur, heavily made up and wearing a large tika, she was also very exotic to foreigners. And Jorge, damn him, loved the exotic. She had gone from one partner to another, vivacious till the end, as Bhagwan grew progressively more bored and deafened by the loud rhythm of the music. His idea of a party was a few, select friends, some drinks, a well-cooked Indian meal with kababs and freshly made rotis hot from the kitchen, a sympathetic hostess coaxing food onto her guests' plates, quiet talk and finally to bed at a reasonable hour, "fed up and fulfilled" as the saying went, in Indian–English. These foreign buffets serving strange fish no sensible person had ever heard of – baby barracuda and octopus in its own ink! – and meat running with blood and pretentious titbits like caviar and foie gras. They can have it, he thought, give me dal-roti any day. Right now, he would have settled for just a hot cup of tea or coffee but it was obvious that he was not going to get any.

"That wretched girl has gone gaga," Sheela stormed. "Breakfast is nowhere near ready and she keeps bawling and saying that Jorge has been murdered in the night and that the police will beat up her sister. Have you heard the like of this?"

"Murdered?" Bhagwan looked incredulous.

"Yes, stabbed. After that lovely party. It's ghastly if it is true, but how can it be? We were among the last to go and he was fine. Look, I'll be late for the dentist if I don't go with you. You can get a cup of coffee at office, can't you?" She grabbed her bag and rushed from the room, calling to him to hurry up.

Bhagwan stood, staring after her. Surely she should be more upset, he thought. How could she take such news in her stride? She had spent most of the night in Jorge's arms. In his mind he could still see a series of images of Sheela: a languid look on her face as she and Jorge executed an Argentinean tango while a circle of admiring guests watched and applauded, later gyrating to a deafening disco beat as the lights in the garden went on and off in a maddening imitation of a discotheque – and late, late in the night snuggling close to Jorge in an old-fashioned fox-trot. And now, barely a few hours later, she could not spare a thought for him and the only thing on her mind seemed to be the damned dentist.

The palatial residence of the Count Jorge de la Bolla, an enormous house, was surrounded by high walls. From the street it was impossible to get any idea of the magnificence which lay beyond: the splendour of the old Spanish colonial architecture, the many large salons leading from one to another, full of fine old furniture, antique treasures and works of art. A large patio with a fountain was surrounded by a deep verandah and behind its arches lay the cool bedrooms. The garden was vast, built on many terraced levels and full of rare shrubs, flowering trees, unusual giant cacti, an orchid house, a swimming pool and two old-fashioned summer houses.

The police were already at work. A large van and several official cars were parked outside the massive wrought-iron gates of the mansion. Armed policemen were much in evidence. The Police Commissioner himself was directing the activities which follow violent death and telephone wires were buzzing as newspapers and magnates of industry clamoured for news. Count Jorge had been no ordinary individual. His wealth alone raised him above his fellow men but besides this he had been very glamorous, a charismatic emblem of romantic San Felice. Here was a crime that would make headlines the world over.

Who could have murdered him? Jorge was fabulously wealthy so there had been much envy regarding his position; he may have had enemies among the multitude of San Felice's less fortunate citizens. He was madly attractive to women, so husbands had been critical. Some whispered that his inclinations were not limited to girls, so some woman may have been infuriated. The Police Commissioner summed up the situation in his statement to an excited set of reporters when he said, "This is a complex puzzle." He added, "But we will find our man."

San Felice was the capital of a small country in Latin America. It was not as well known as some other countries of the region for vast quantities of oil or the splendid remains of a pre-Columbian culture, but it had all the charm and inconvenience of an old world provincial town. The Indian embassy residence was situated in a street lined with trees – locally called *Tulipa de la India*, not after India but in recognition of '*los Indios*', the original inhabitants of San Felice. The trees were in bloom now with an abundance of flame-coloured clusters, giving the quiet residential area a very spectacular look.

Normally an early riser, Savitri, the Indian ambassadress, had overslept. The late hour of their return from Jorge's party was not the only reason. For once, her never-flagging energy had failed her and she felt tired and sluggish, unable to face her morning routine of yoga exercises. She arrived at last in the dining room dressed and ready for a busy day, to find her daughter lounging in her dressing gown with a cup of black coffee. Savitri was a middle-aged woman with hair dyed jet black. Her face, which had been insipidly pretty in youth, had changed through the years and though still pleasant, was stern with character. A lifetime of making decisions and ruling a household had given her several of the attributes of a not very benevolent monarch.

"Really, Mona," she said in her strident voice, eyeing the black coffee as well as the pink quilted dressing gown. "Where is your glass of milk? And how many times have I told you not to come down dressed like this? Heaven knows what the servants think. How will you ever control them when you have a home of your own?"

"Good morning, Mama," Mona replied. "I'm sorry, but it was so late last night and I'm not even properly awake yet. Anyway I don't have classes today."

Mona was nineteen years old, not pretty but with the appeal of youth and the beautiful almond-shaped eyes of many Indian girls. Her long black hair was carelessly braided.

Savitri looked at her daughter and thought, "Thank God Anil is coming today." It was time Mona was married off. A few weeks ago Savitri had heard that the son of one of her childhood friends was in the United States and with her usual presence of mind, she had written to the young man inviting him to come and stay with his old aunty. Anil had accepted and was due to arrive on the evening flight.

"You remember, don't you, that Anil arrives today?" she asked Mona.

"I can hardly forget, Mama, you keep reminding me several times a day!" Mona replied.

"Well, child, he is a nice boy, pots of money in the family and it is time you were settled," Savitri chided. As Mona started to giggle she continued, "Nothing to laugh about. Both your brothers came to me when they wanted to marry and asked me to choose nice girls for them. Don't you remember how they said, 'Mama, only you will know the right girl for me.' And I must say, I did manage to find each one the right bride. Look how happy they both are." She thought of her two pretty daughters-in-law. College graduates, very well brought up and so well-connected. One was the only daughter of a wealthy industrialist and the other had relatives in high political circles. Most satisfactory. Now only Mona remained but, unlike her brothers, the girl was giving her trouble.

"Mama, I don't want to get married," Mona said, breaking into Savitri's thoughts. Savitri paid no attention. Girls always talked like this. Mona seemed to be developing very willful ways – But it is just *zid*, stubbornness, Savitri said to herself, it will pass. She rang the bell for her lemon juice in hot water. She took it first thing in the morning for her complexion.

Ram Nath entered with the drink on a silver salver, his face funereal. Greeting his mistress, he said in a somber tone, "Bibiji, I have very bad news for you. Jorge Sahib has been stabbed to death."

With the glass of lemon water raised to her mouth, Savitri stared at him and said curtly, "Don't be a fool!" Mona dropped her cup of coffee and, as a dark stain spread over her pink dressing gown, she cried out, "Oh no!" Tears welled up in her eyes and poured down her face.

"Control yourself, Mona," Savitri snapped automatically and began to question Ram Nath. Gulati Singh, the cook, was sent for and came from the kitchen in a dirty apron, with a day's bristle on his face. "Get out of my sight," shouted

Savitri, "and don't come back until you have shaved and put on clean clothes!"

So it was some time before the terrible story, communicated by Conchita, was unfolded and mulled over. It was astounding. Jorge, not so young but so very handsome, so very rich and with so much to live for, stabbed to death! Savitri was appalled. Since their arrival in San Felice they had come to know Jorge well. As a collector of the unusual, he had found them an interesting addition to his circle of friends – and to be considered a friend of Jorge's was social triumph indeed. He knew nothing about India – in fact Asia, as a whole, was to him a distant part of the world filled with dire poverty, foreign in every way. In India, he vaguely knew, there were erotic temple sculptures, the poems of Tagore, mystic philosophy. Then, there were recurring famines, urine therapy and a lot of odd things that made no sense. But he liked the Ambassador and his family, found spicy Indian food delicious and was a frequent guest at the Indian Embassy parties. He was the sort of person who was intrigued by an alien culture without making the least effort to understand it. "Your country fascinates me," he used to tell Indians, going on to say that he thought the *chaprasis* were too delicious – when he meant *chapattis*. He was the kind of man who, if asked about the Himalayas, would answer in an off-hand way, "Loved him, hated her!"

Many Indians felt indignant at Jorge's foolish patter and his frequent references to how much he longed to visit India, if only he were not so sensitive to poverty. Savitri, however, did not mind. She knew well that foreigners were mad. One had to pretend to be at ease with them because it was polite to do so and also, her husband's career demanded it. For herself she yearned for only one thing – the day of her husband's retirement so they could return to familiar surroundings and live in their family home. If a foreigner turned up there he would be a very unusual sight. Yet she had been genuinely fond of Jorge. She found herself thinking, inconsequentially, what a pity it was that he would not grace the reception next week for Republic Day, the Indian national holiday which was the apex of her programme of official entertaining.

Mona sat in a daze, her mind refusing to accept the incredible words that were being repeated with morbid relish by the servants. She tried to make her mind blank. Think of nothing, she kept repeating to herself. But instead, there came into her mind the sudden thought that her riding boots were still lying in a bedroom in Jorge's house.

Much later in the day a beautiful young man with honey-coloured hair staggered from his tousled bed and called imperiously to his valet for coffee. He reached for his silk dressing gown with a blue and crimson paisley design, and switched on the transistor radio on his bedside table. The midday news bulletin had already begun and his unbelieving ears heard a disembodied voice announce that the police would leave no stone unturned in finding the murderer of the Count de la Bolla. With an anguished, choking sound he fell onto his bed and when, a little later, his valet entered with a silver tray of coffee and cream, it was to find his young master in a paroxysm of grief.

TWO

Police in the Embassy

When Bhagwan got to the Chancery he proceeded ponderously up the staircase past the pictures of Indian monuments in the hall, until he reached his office. He rang for his personal assistant and Nair entered with a cheerful greeting and a pad and pencil for dictation. Bhagwan collapsed into his chair. "Get me coffee immediately," he grunted, "I haven't had any at home."

Nair had strong views on wives who let husbands leave for office without breakfast. His own comely little wife would not dream of such a thing, and she always had his lunch box ready for him no matter how early he had to leave. But none of this showed in his face as he left the room. Very soon he returned with a cup of instant coffee, half full of condensed milk and fortified with several spoons of sugar. Again he had his pad ready but Bhagwan, after taking a gulp of the steaming coffee, pulled the phone towards him and began to dial. "Later, later," he said impatiently to Nair and then, as the line was connected, he spoke into the phone.

"Have you heard the news?"

"What news?"

"Jorge has been killed."

"What – how do you know?"

"It's news, everyone is talking about it. And let me tell you here and now that enough is enough. I am not standing for any more..."

"My dear chap..."

"Don't you dare 'my dear chap' me, you swine. I'm through with you." With that he slammed down the receiver, breathing hard, and grabbed his coffee cup.

Bhagwan had been under great strain for some time. Due to circumstances beyond his control, he had had to succumb to the threats of a blackguard. He had tried to avoid the situation; blackmail was a dirty word anywhere, but in diplomatic life it could lead to grave complications. He had no intention of compromising his convictions or doing anything that could possibly be construed as treason. His humourless "my country right or wrong" attitude would have made it impossible for him to do so in any case. So far, in fact, he had not done anything at all since he got the threat. But unhappily the threat hanging over him concerned not his activities but those of his wife – activities that were not only scandalous but humiliating to his pride and not to be tolerated. Bhagwan had had to agree, in principle, to pay for silence and the cost to his morale had been heavy. Suppressed in some subconscious layer of his being was the memory of something unbearably painful: a memory of himself as a shy teenager entering unexpectedly into a dim room on a summer afternoon to see Didi, his elder sister, and a man who was not his brother-in-law. Although his memory had clouded over the years, he could still smell the fragrance of *khus*, Didi's favourite summer perfume; he could see a pale blue cotton sari discarded in a limp heap on the floor, a dark hand cupping Didi's full, golden breast. He had been rooted to the floor for what seemed like an endless amount of time but had finally managed to leave silently, without his presence being observed. And though he had long ceased to be haunted by this picture, there were times when he could not help remembering it. In recent weeks when the memory came unbidden, in place of Didi he would see Sheela.

He could have beaten his wife for infidelity, he supposed, as another man might have done. But that was not his way. He could not even mention the matter to her, so deep was his hurt. But now the seducer, as he rather dramatically thought of him, was dead and he was a free man. He was in no doubt at all that Jorge had been having an affair with Sheela. A dozen things pointed to it – the way he kept calling her "*mi vida*" and "*mi amor*" for one. He did the same with other women, as was the custom of his country, but Bhagwan was certain that he caught a special light in Jorge's eyes when he addressed Sheela in this manner. Then there was the gift of a bottle of expensive French perfume at Christmas, nestling in a basket of yellow roses. Often the phone would ring and Sheela would answer in a soft voice and return looking pleased. Who but Jorge could she be talking to? Even the way the wretched fellow kissed her hand! No, no, it was obvious that he was her lover.

Although it was bag day, the most hectic day in the week, Jorge's death and not the chancery work was foremost in all minds. The local employees were frankly bereaved at the loss. They did not know Jorge of course, but avidly read of his various activities in the society pages. The other members of the Embassy did not care one way or another but were curious because the Count was an influential man and a friend of their boss. The Ambassador had verified the sad news and several of his colleagues had been on the phone. Many had attended Jorge's last party and they were aghast – also, bewildered at the manner of the crime. Why, they asked? And also, who? And when? For the guests had stayed late, well after midnight and in fact the younger crowd had been threatening to stay for a breakfast of bacon and eggs when the older guests had started to make a move.

Nobody seemed to know for certain when the last guest

had left the illuminated garden. A sleepy waiter had discovered Jorge's body lying in a pool of blood. The police had been called and a statement was made that the death had been effected by stabbing, though there was no sign of the murder weapon or any other clue as to the perpetrator of the crime.

Late in the afternoon, as the Ambassador was signing various letters to be included in the bag, the Commissioner of Police telephoned to ask for a meeting as soon as possible. "Come at once, if you like," the Ambassador told him. He had met the Commissioner frequently at official functions but did not know him well. He wondered what he wanted to see him about.

The Commissioner of Police was a very important person, related by birth to the oldest families in the country. He was a man of means and did not need to take on the arduous duties he had to perform in his office, but when his President had asked for his help, he had been proud to comply. His wife had died several years ago and his eleven children were long married and had scattered. He enjoyed his job and it kept him busy.

Presently he was ushered into the Ambassador's room and, with many apologies, he took an easy chair and refused the offer of tea. He was a tall, well-built man with a mane of thick grey hair and a neat beard. In official life he was known to be a tiger but in his social relationships he was suave and could be counted on to be discreet when discretion was called for.

"Excuse me, Excellency," he said, rather ill-at-ease for so urbane a man, "but something urgent has come up and I had to see you immediately."

"Of course, of course," replied the Ambassador. "Anything I can do to help you… we shall not be disturbed."

"Your Excellency, it is a most delicate matter, but you understand I must do my duty."

"Please explain yourself, Commissioner," the Ambassador said, mystified.

"It is this terrible matter of the Count's murder. My men have been at his residence since morning and it has been reported to me that a pair of riding boots, allegedly belonging to your daughter, have been found in a most compromising place."

"Good heavens," exclaimed the Ambassador, in surprise. "What do you mean? What compromising place can riding boots possibly be found in? And how do you know that they belong to my daughter?"

The Commissioner shifted in his chair. Matters with diplomats were tricky and furthermore he had to deal with an Indian – they were touchy and had strange customs, he knew, and he wondered how to tell this man with the inscrutable face that his daughter could well turn out to be a murder suspect. He cleared his throat and said, "Excellency, it is a delicate matter, as I said. It is known that your daughter went riding with the Count yesterday. She was seen in the house with him afterwards and the boots," he went on in a lower voice, "were found under the Count's bed."

The Ambassador blanched. He was a mild man in general but this allegation against his daughter was not to be borne. Jumping up he said, "Impossible!" He paced up and down the room in agitation, and turning to face the Commissioner again, he repeated, "Impossible!"

The Commissioner looked away. He hesitated at having to hurt a father's sensibilities. Even in a matter of crime and duty, one should be a gentleman. "If I can have a word with the young lady, I am sure a satisfactory answer will be found," he said at last.

"We will go at once to my house," the Ambassador replied. Leaving the bag's letters unsigned he went downstairs, saying in a shaken voice that his daughter was a child and he hoped the Commissioner would be gentle with her.

The official Mercedes, flying the Indian flag, sped through the town and turned at the embassy gateway where the three lions of the Indian government seal glowed with polish. Ram

Nath opened the front door even before the car had come to a complete stop.

In the garden the deep green lawn was enhanced by the coloured dresses of half a dozen women who were taking tea with the ambassadress. Sitting under a shady tree in wicker chairs, they presented a pretty picture and the Commissioner, being a ladies' man, paused to admire them. But the Ambassador hurried him into the house and asked Ram Nath to send for his daughter. "Baby has gone out," was the reply. The Ambassador felt great relief at the postponement of a confrontation. He needed time to think. The Commissioner, with further polite apologies, decided to leave. "I shall be in touch with Your Excellency," he said and, though he was most amiable, the Ambassador thought there was a subtle change in his manner. Was there a touch of steel in his voice? He was apprehensive. What the hell had Mona been up to and where the devil was she?

Mona had left the house right after lunch. On bag days her father never came home for lunch and she and her mother had a light meal. This was soon over and she felt so unhappy and restless that she had to get out of the house. She knew that her mother had people coming to tea and would expect her to be around and make small talk, which would inevitably revolve around the horror of Jorge's killing. She could not bear the thought of it.

Since morning, Mona had felt thoroughly disoriented. A violent death is always shocking but for it to happen to someone she had known so well! She clearly remembered her first meeting with Jorge. It had been at a dinner party at a western European embassy. Very elegant: butlers in white gloves and sophisticated talk in several languages. She had felt a fool being there. She had been reluctant to go when the invitation came, but her mother had insisted. "Mona, you must learn to behave in society," she had said sternly. "After all, you may marry a foreign service officer one day!" God forbid, Mona had thought.

Before dinner while everyone sipped aperitifs and chattered gaily about nothing, Mona had been tongue-tied, drinking her tomato juice in nervous gulps. She turned around and saw a man looking at her with an amused expression. Coming up to her, he raised one eyebrow and said, "Deadly bore, these parties, aren't they?" Mona was surprised into stammering, "I'm scared of all these grand people!" He laughed and told her there was no need: in her beautiful sari she looked grander than anyone in the room. Introducing himself he asked her, "What are you doing, going to college?"

Hardly knowing what she was saying, Mona replied, "I'm not clever enough."

He smiled, raising one eyebrow again and said, "Well, there are many more interesting things to do than go to college."

This was a new idea to Mona. "Really?" she asked. "What, for instance?"

"Let me think," he answered. "You could do a course on the history of art, or learn to weave or to play the guitar. Or perhaps you could marry a maharaja and invite me to your palace for a tiger shoot."

Mona was delighted. "We don't have maharajas any more," she confided, "and we are trying to save our tigers, but I hope you will come and visit me in India one day."

Jorge was enchanted with the young girl, so different from the worldly teenagers of his own country. When he heard that she was fond of horses and rode well, he asked her to visit his stables and to exercise one of his horses. To Mona it was a dream come true. She knew that Jorge belonged to another world, one far removed from her own. He looked like a movie star and in every way seemed more like a hero in a romantic novel than someone who could be her friend. Yet that was just what he became. Why, it was due to him that her parents had allowed her to take a course in ceramics at the Academy of Handicrafts. Her mother had not liked the idea, saying that a BA degree was essential. But her father had approved and she loved her classes and the feel of the clay. Also, thanks to Jorge, she could have a ride every morning. Only yesterday she had been on a cross-country gallop with Jorge. It was not often she had the opportunity of riding with him because he was busy with many things and away from San Felice for months at a time. But yesterday he had come into the stable while she was saddling Martini, the chestnut gelding she usually rode.

Afterwards she had gone home with him. She had gone to have a wash, pulled off her riding boots and changed into the sneakers she had with her. Jorge had insisted that she have breakfast with him and they had been summoned to the meal by his family butler. Mona had been a bit nervous of the butler; he was not at all like Ram Nath – more like a count himself. On the terrace facing the garden, a wrought-iron table had been laid for two with crisply starched linen, iced grapefruit halves and a score of covered silver dishes. The stately butler kept serving these, whispering their names in Mona's ear, *huevos revueltos*, *frijoles refritos*, grilled kidneys, croissants, *tortillas de harina* and so on. But though she was hungry as a bear she could hardly swallow a morsel; the thrill of her first tête-à-tête with Jorge was too much for her.

As for Jorge, he had lounged there drinking coffee with milk and cinnamon and crunching an imported apple while he talked casually of this and that. Impossible to remember what he said; all she could recall was the contented feeling of being with him. After the meal was over he had told her to hop into his sports model Alfa-Romeo and had driven her home. All day, she had been happy and excited at the prospect of his big party in the evening.

It was while dressing for the evening that she had suddenly remembered that her passport had been in her jacket pocket that morning. Better keep it on my dressing table so I can send it to the office tomorrow, she thought. But putting her hand into both the pockets of the riding jacket, she found they were empty. Oh well, it must be somewhere or other, she could not be bothered with it at this time. She continued dressing and put on a very pretty *gharara*, new, made of green silk with a gold design woven into it. She was pleased with it and forgot about her passport.

But since the morning she had been worrying about her boots as well as the missing passport. Obviously she could not go to Jorge's house now, with the police around. What to do? She wandered aimlessly downstairs and into the hall. The telephone was ringing and she picked it up.

"Hello?"

"Mona, is that you? Look, I'm coming to pick you up, meet me at the gate."

It was Kwame. Thank goodness. She ran out of the house without a word to anyone, happy to be able to escape.

Kwame was a young journalist doing something or other with the U.N. They had met at a cocktail party at his embassy, a west African country. Seeing a young girl in a sari standing alone and shy in the midst of an animated throng of people, Kwame had gone up to her. Lots of Indians had a thing about colour, he had been told, and he thought it would be amusing to tease her with his attention.

"What about a drink?" he asked.

"May I have a ginger ale, please?" she answered.

"Better make it brandy ginger – that's our national drink," he said with a grin and gave the order to a passing waiter. Presently Mona had a tall, cold glass in her hand. It had a strange flavour. Deafened by the crescendo of sound around them, she turned to him and said, "This ginger ale tastes funny!"

"Well, it's made in my country," he answered with a broad grin, then relenting at her bewildered expression, added, "It's got brandy in it."

"Brandy! My mother would faint if she knew I was drinking alcohol!" But Mona continued to sip the drink, looking quite pleased with herself. Before long she felt a warm glow and listening to Kwame's flippant talk she realized that she no longer felt shy. In fact she felt more at ease with him than with most people she had met since coming to San Felice. They chatted happily throughout the evening.

Savitri, coming from another salon and looking around the room with her party smile, had been horrified to see Mona giggling at something a young African was bending to say in her ear. We may be at an African embassy party, she thought indignantly, but there is no need for Mona to get so chummy. She pushed her way through the solid mass of guests and almost dragged Mona away from Kwame. Not completely, though. Kwame and Mona continued to meet at friends' homes and sometimes he took her out in his bright yellow Beatle. The first time she saw the car she refused to get into anything that was such a garish colour. But Kwame just laughed. "Black and yellow is a smart combination, girl," he told her. "Besides, I'm the Yellow Peril in disguise!"

Now as they drove down the tulip tree avenue towards the town, Mona started to tell Kwame about her terrible day: first the shock of Jorge's death and since then the worry over her riding boots. "I often do change into comfy shoes after riding, you know," she said. "I'm not really worried about the boots. But what about my passport? Whatever can have happened to it?"

"I've never heard of anyone going riding with a passport. Surely you have a diplomatic identity card you can carry."

"Of course, silly, but I took my passport because I had to send it to the office for a visa. Then I must have forgotten all about it. I just put it in my jacket pocket as a reminder!"

"You are a bird-brain, aren't you," said Kwame. You'll

probably come across it next time you open a drawer to take out a hanky or something."

"I only use Kleenex," replied Mona pertly. But she began to worry again. She had already looked through all her drawers and her closet, and had not found the passport. What was Mama going to say?

THREE

Enter Anil

In the busy commercial section of town there was a tiny but exclusive boutique run by two young women. Gloria and Francisca were distant cousins and belonged to an old, respected family no longer as rich as it had once been. They were an enterprising pair and had not wanted to waste their lives in shabby gentility; but neither was trained to do a job and suitable husbands had not yet come their way. Family connections could certainly have found them employment of some sort but they decided to try their luck with the growing number of tourists finding their way to San Felice, and to start a boutique which specialized in local handicrafts. They were patronized at first by family and close friends but very soon their clientele expanded and they were able to rent a small room in the fashionable shopping arcade of downtown San Felice.

Gloria, a slim brunette, was one of the chief attractions of the boutique. Her vivacious manner and flair for style made her a favourite with the men who wandered in to look for gifts for their wives. Francisca, older and stolid, had a good head for business and kept the books. She did the ordering and was the heart of the little shop. Together, they ran La Boutique with efficiency. They were taking a coffee break in a small alcove behind a screen painted with red, turquoise and black quetzacotls – the beautiful birds whose plumage had adorned the headdress of ancient Mayan chiefs – when the door opened with a jingling of bells. Pepe entered, the sun glinting on his honey-coloured hair.

"My dears, coffee, what heaven!" he cried. "A cup for little me?"

Francisca noticed, as she rose to fetch another pottery mug, that Pepe was looking ghastly. He was very pale and his eyes were heavy, as if he had been crying. Instead of his usual velvet trousers of pink or chartreuse, he was wearing a rather formal corduroy suit and a black tie for Jorge. He took a sip from the mug of coffee handed to him.

"Darlings, I've come to get your advice. Should I go to the police?"

"Police? Whatever for?" The girls were surprised.

"I'm beside myself because of this tragedy. The destruction of someone as wonderful as Jorge! I feel I must do something. After all," he continued with a glance at Gloria, "he was a very, very special friend of mine. I may have information that will help the police."

"What information, Pepe?" asked Francisca. Gloria said tartly, "He was a special friend of all of us. Our families have known each other for ages. When I think how full of life he was only last night! I begged Francisca to close the shop today in his memory but she refused to listen to me." She added, "I've been crying all day – I just came here a little while ago because I couldn't bear to be alone at home any longer."

"Now now, Gloria," Francisca's sensible tone was like that of a good nanny, "don't brood about it. It's better to keep working. It's the height of the tourist season and I made several sales this morning."

"How could you...?" Gloria's big blue eyes filled with tears. "None of you can understand... you don't know what I went through when I heard the news... you don't know what Jorge meant to me!"

Francisca looked disapproving and Pepe sceptical. Both knew that Gloria, much younger than Jorge, had been crazy about him ever since he had danced with her at her *cinze anos*; her coming-out party.

"He and I were very, very close," she continued, her voice breaking, lips trembling. The doorbell jangled again and in walked Mona and Kwame, calling out, "Anyone home?" Francisca jumped up in relief. She hated scenes as much as Gloria seemed to revel in them. She went to embrace Mona and saw that her eyes, too, were red with crying.

"It's good to see you Mona," she said. "I see you are as upset as we are over this terrible news."

"I just can't believe it," Mona replied. "Kwame didn't know Jorge but I've been telling him what a fabulous person he was. Who could have wanted to kill him?"

"Any number of people," Kwame answered, in his deep voice. "Some revolutionary, for instance, or one of the many under-privileged people you all keep ignoring in your country."

Francisca gave him a disapproving look. She did not like all this talk about poor people and communists. "Pepe wants to go to the police and offer to help them," she said, to create a diversion.

"It's not a question of helping," Pepe said, waving his beautiful hands. "I know what actually happened. I feel I killed him with my own two hands... you people just don't understand..." His voice was rising in hysteria and everyone stared at him, alarmed.

"How could you know, Pepe?" Kwame inquired, in his characteristic no-nonsense manner.

"I do, I tell you, I know. I can't tell you more, it's a private matter but I do know and I'll treasure my memories always, until I die. You can't make me forget them, nobody can..."

"Good heavens, Pepe, do get a hold of yourself. What are you talking about? If anyone else heard you, you'd be in trouble with the police."

But Pepe had already flung himself out of the door and as the bells jangled once again, the three women looked at one another in dismay. They all knew Pepe and his strange moods but this one seemed to be out of the ordinary. And where did the police come into it – how could he help them?

"Will someone tell me what that was all about?" asked Kwame. No one could give him a satisfactory answer.

Sheela, lying in contented abandon in the arms of a stocky, swarthy man with a small moustache, stroked his cheek and whispered, "That awful murder seems to belong to another life when I'm with you."

"My little chicken," murmured her lover. He too was contented, but now he wanted her to go home. He had important business affairs to see to in the afternoon.

"Why can't we always be like this," she said plaintively, starting to caress his broad chest. For obvious reasons, he thought, but he continued to whisper sweet nothings into her ear. He still needed her and the fact that she was utterly bewitched by him was all for the good. In fact it was essential for his future plans. He covered her face with little kisses and rumpled her hair, and finally coaxed her to leave the king-size bed they lay on.

"You know, chicken," he said with a melting look, "I want to be with you all the time but I have a board meeting later. And anyway, you must be careful."

"Oh bother, what does it matter? Besides it's bag day and Bhagwan won't be home for ages and ages."

"Still, chicken, for my sake." He slapped her shapely rump.

Presently he was alone. He pressed a button and soft

mood music filled the room. Then he took a shower, dressed carefully and went to the writing table. He took a pad of plain white paper and started to print in childish letters: ALL SET PROCEED AS ARRANGED. He put the paper into a cheap envelope and addressed it to a PO Box number at the General Post Office.

Everything was working out well, according to plan – in fact, even better than he had anticipated. Frankly, he had been prepared for a long wait but either chance or the will of the gods had worked in his favour. Only last night at Jorge's jamboree he had happened to wander into a room. Surely he was led by fate into that particular room for he had never a thought in his head but to find the toilet. But on the way there, he saw a pair of riding boots by a chaise longue. One had fallen across the other and automatically he crossed the room to straighten it. He could not stand seeing shoes lie awry; something to do with a childhood remembrance of his mother's superstition that such a sight meant death in the family. As he bent down to pick up the offending boot his hand touched something hard. He drew out a little red book – an Indian diplomatic passport, belonging to none other than that schoolgirl daughter of the ass of an ambassador! He looked at Mona's picture. It could be any non-descript girl, passport photos were seldom good. Height 5 ft. 3 in., weight 103 lbs, no distinguishing marks, black hair and eyes. Luck was certainly with him. He pocketed the passport and went to the toilet. Then, for the fun of it, he took the boots across the empty patio into a large gold and cream bedroom which he guessed belonged to Jorge. With a snigger he tossed the boots under the canopied bed and returned to the garden lit with fairy lights. Waiters scurried by with tempting canapés and glasses of champagne. He took one that was offered to him and went to watch the dancers who were swaying to the rhythm of a marimba band. Sipping the Dom Perignon, he looked around at the elite of San Felice who were the guests of the great Count and congratulated himself on his entry into this select gathering.

His life had not always been one of luxury, attending the parties of the playboy set. He had run away from home while still a child and worked at every job that came his way. He had known hunger and deprivation but had been determined to make good somehow. As always, luck had been with him and here he was, in his thirties, with an excellent position and bank balance, plenty of native sense and a face that had a curious attraction for women despite its ugliness. His business was one of import-export, a legitimate concern which gave him scope for other more lucrative ways of enlarging his fortune. He had done good business with watches and transistors but now he was on to something really big. It was with this new venture in mind that he had started an affair with Sheela. He needed a little diplomatic help and she obviously needed something her stick of a husband could not provide. Too bad about the murder of old Jorge but he did not think it would affect his schemes. They lay in another direction after all.

At the embassy residence, Savitri waited alone for Anil's arrival. Her mind was full of wedding plans. It never entered her head that Anil and Mona might not shortly be married and she was envisioning the *mandap*, supported by banana plants and decorated with garlands of marigolds. Mona would wear a sari of traditional bridal pink with gold embroidery.

She would have to start making lists of wedding guests soon. It would not do to leave any important person off the guest list. She went on to think of the dinner menu; a buffet perhaps, so there could be more variety and a good display. Where was Mona? Her happy train of thought was interrupted when she remembered that Mona had been absent all afternoon. The child was getting out of hand. Disappearing like that after lunch without a word to anyone! And her husband had asked her how it was that Mona's riding boots had been found under Jorge's bed! Good heavens, what a shock she had had. If she didn't know that Mona was a shy little mouse she would have been most perturbed. And anyway, Jorge was a gentleman. She had soothed her husband – men got so upset about things – and decided to give Mona a good yelling. It was the only way to deal with the situation. She would soon find out all about the boots.

Meanwhile, the Ambassador was shut up in his study, mulling over the strange events of the day over a scotch on the rocks. His wife kept all alcoholic drinks under lock and key, to be served only when there were guests, and the bunch of keys were tucked into the waistband of her sari just like any good Indian housewife. But over the years, the Ambassador had learnt to fend for himself and he usually had a bottle of single malt hidden away in a drawer. Sometimes he used to drop in on his Counsellor, a dull dog but a hard worker, and Sheela always made him welcome and gave him a drink. He believed it was a good thing to fraternize with young people. He was certainly not an alcoholic but there are days, he used to say to himself, when a man needs a drink and the quiet of his study. Tonight was certainly such a time. The scotch calmed him and he was not so worried now about Mona's indiscretion and the policeman's hints. In any case, Savitri would soon get to the bottom of the mystery of the boots. She always managed to do what she wanted. He had no doubt that she would arrange a marriage between Anil and Mona as well.

It was already dark when Mona came hurrying in. Savitri heard the front door open and came into the hall, thundering, "Where have you been all day?"

"With Kwame," Mona mumbled as she ran to the staircase.

"My God! That creature! Have you no shame? And Anil is expected at any moment. You were supposed to see to flowers in his room. And you know I wanted you to go to the airport to receive him. Now go and make yourself presentable at once. There are important matters to discuss but they'll have to wait until tomorrow. Hurry up, now!"

With a sullen look at her mother, Mona went up the stairs to her room and took her time washing her face and then combing her long hair. When she returned to the drawing room Anil was already there, sitting with her parents and telling them the latest Delhi gossip. He had recently written a best-selling political mystery called *Death by Defection*, an ingenious tale in which the victim succumbs to a poisoned laddu, eaten after an official swearing-in ceremony at Rashtrapati Bhawan. The young author had just presented a copy of his book to the Ambassador, who was taken aback at the prospect of reading this type of literature. Ram Nath was passing whiskey, soda and glasses of fruit juice around, and little bowls of cashew nuts and potato wafers were on the coffee table. As Mona entered, her mother turned a smiling face towards her and said in her party voice, "Ah, here comes my little girl. She has turned into a young lady since you last saw her, Anil. I expect she has been making herself pretty for you, my dear boy!"

With a dark look at her mother, Mona went and sat on a pouf. "Mona doesn't need to make herself pretty for me," said Anil, with his engaging grin. "Hi. Remember how we used to run up and down the corridors of Ashoka Hotel exchanging the shoes left to be cleaned outside the doors?" Mona began to giggle.

"Yes I do," she said. "And also the times we turned the cards on the doors around from DO NOT DISTURB to PLEASE CLEAN THE ROOM." They laughed, remembering all the wicked things they had done one winter many years ago when Anil had come with his parents to Delhi. Mona was much younger than Anil and she had loved following his lead in all their games. It was ages since they had met but he seemed just as nice. She looked at him appraisingly. He was quite tall, a little overweight but still nice-looking. It's not going to be at all bad having Anil here, especially now when everything is so sick, she thought. He had always been fun to be with and she was pretty sure he did not want to marry her. The two continued to kid around as other memories of mischief and merrymaking came back to them.

Savitri listened to their childish talk with an indulgent smile. Perhaps not a pink sari, she thought, Mona is too dark. Pity she doesn't have my fair complexion. Peach will suit her better and she can wear an emerald set with it – dangling earrings and a heavy gold and emerald necklace, she decided happily.

While these pleasant thoughts came and went in Savitri's mind the talk turned to what Anil should see and do while in San Felice. The Ambassador, whom Anil had always called uncle, did not approve of Savitri's innuendos and remarks regarding Mona and Anil. These matters called for finesse not a bulldozer – delicacy was essential. He started telling Anil of the remains of Mayan civilization to be seen not far from San Felice.

"But first you have to see the museum," he said.

"Museum?" Anil sounded alarmed at the thought but Mona assured him he would enjoy it. The Ambassador told Anil it was unique and said that he had recommended to the government that Indian museologists should make a study of it.

They continued to chat about this and that until Ram Nath came in to announce that dinner was served. They all got up and went into the dining room where the fragrance of roganjosh held the promise of a delicious meal.

FOUR

Boots and Intrigues

It was Sunday and Bhagwan had slept soundly and left for the Ambassador's residence after a hearty breakfast of cornflakes, juice and eggs rancheros, followed by several slices of toast and jam and cups of tea. Full as he was, he would have preferred the kind of breakfast his mother used to prepare, especially on Sunday mornings. She had always cooked up delicious aloo paranthas, to be eaten with pickles and dahi followed by crisp, hot jalebis, Bhagwan's favourite sweet, with a glass of steaming boiled milk. There was always toast as well, with homemade jam and honey and fruit. An orange would be peeled, or an apple cut into neat slices; his mother would persuade her son to try to eat just a little more. Here they had no Indian cook to make those treats and Sheela could not be bothered. She probably did not know how to prepare them. He had to eat whatever Conchita could make and her forte seemed to be eggs rancheros, which was getting boring.

The Ambassador had phoned in the morning and asked Bhagwan to come over to discuss matters pertaining to a delegation that was expected from India. At the residence, Bhagwan was led into the study by Ram Nath and he stood looking at the daggers which covered one wall. An odd thing to collect, he always thought. Several were Indian, from various states and of varying quality. There was one of fine chased silver. Two were from Nepal, one of them studded with coloured stones. There was a mean-looking Gurkha knife, two or three of Arab creation – Moroccan, or Tunisian. There were African spears and daggers too, some very primitive. He had asked the Ambassador about them once and had been given an hour-long lecture on the origin of each, where it had been found and how much bargaining lay behind the purchase of every one of them. He had been thoroughly bored at the end of it.

"But isn't it dangerous to have weapons like these on the walls? Do they need a license? Anyone could walk off with one," he had remarked. "My dear Bhagwan, why should anyone take them? Anyhow, they are quite blunt you know. As modern weapons they are quite useless. I like them for their workmanship, whether sophisticated or primitive. For me they are things of beauty. In any case they are fully insured."

Looking at them now, as he waited for the Ambassador, Bhagwan wondered what made him think they were blunt. Had he felt them? And how could he think some of those hideous pieces were beautiful – he doubted if there was even one antique piece among them.

"Well, Bhagwan." The strident voice made Bhagwan turn around with a start. "I didn't know," said Savitri, "that you were here." She stood in the doorway and stared at him. He wondered how long she had been standing there.

"I came over to discuss some matters with H.E.," he said. Savitri liked her husband to be called H.E. by the staff. She herself never called him by his name when speaking to other people. She referred to him as "the Ambassador" or sometimes simply as "He", like a traditional Hindu wife who never takes the name of her husband.

"He told me we are to have a big delegation from India," she continued. "Will there be any MPs in it?"

"Yes indeed, it is a parliamentary delegation," Bhagwan said. He saw a look of consternation appear on her face.

"I do hope there will not be any trouble," she said. "In our last post, an MP who came to dinner got very angry. He thumped the table so hard that he broke the glass top. That was in Syria. Oh, what a lot of trouble there was! And the landlord was very angry because we couldn't replace the glass top – quality has gone down you know and that old heavy glass just isn't made any more." Bhagwan looked at her with disapproval. MPs were sacrosanct to him.

But Savitri did not notice. She had wandered down memory lane, remembering various MPs. "When we were in Moscow I remember going with HE to the airport to meet a delegation, and when the leader of the delegation arrived he was wearing an embroidered Kashimiri dressing gown and earmuffs! Can you imagine?"

"Why earmuffs?" asked Bhagwan, who was not surprised at the dressing gown.

"There was snow on the ground," Savitri told him coldly, and went off to the kitchen to look for the cook and inform him that VIPs would be present at the Republic Day reception and that he should outdo himself in the preparation of the feast for that day.

In the kitchen, Gulati Singh was already preparing samosas for the big event. Lupita, the elderly maid, was helping him by rolling out thin circles of dough while he filled them with the potato mixture and deftly shaped them into triangles.

"When there is trouble in my village and the police come around we always make a vow, a *manat*, to the goddess," he told Ram Nath over his shoulder. "It is the only thing that helps. Now you tell me that the big police chief has been here and I am sure others will come. Mark my words. I am going to tell Bibiji to make a *manat* when I see her."

"You will only be called a fool," said Ram Nath. "She is always shouting at you."

"Let her shout. She is my father and my mother and I never take notice when she is angry with me. It is her right. I am her child."

"Some child," muttered Ram Nath. Gulati tossed another samosa on to the growing pile and said, "What's the matter with you?"

Ram Nath threw down the polishing cloth with which he was shining the silver and said in exasperation, "You are such a fool, how have they kept you so long?"

"Yes, I have been with them for years," Gulati laughed happily. "That time when I was sick with malaria in Africa I thought it would be the end. I kept seeing a ghost – a black nude woman – but she was a good ghost and I told Bibiji she meant no harm. Then I went home to my village for my leave and the village priest told me to pour five kilos of buttermilk over my head every single day. And I was cured! You see how well I am now. I will cook at Baby's wedding."

"My God," said Ram Nath. "If you had drunk all that buttermilk it would have improved your brain." Really, Gulati was too stupid to be true.

"Budiya," Gulati called gaily to Lupita. He was utterly unaware of Ram Nath's irritation. "Roll faster or we will be at this task all day."

"Why do you call me Budhiya, you know my name is Lupita?" the maid asked.

"In my country, budiya means a señorita," said Gulati and burst into a cackle of laughter. Lupita, who was well past forty, preened, and Ram Nath left the room in disgust.

The samosa making continued and was soon done.

In a part of the town not usually frequented by Indian embassy personnel, a conference was taking place in a small room over a wine shop. The room was plainly furnished with plastic covered chairs and a large round table. On this was a bottle of Nuits St. Georges and a few wine glasses. One of the men seated at the table was a swarthy, thick-set man, conservatively dressed. The others were more casually attired and one wore a pair of faded, patched blue jeans and a dirty army jacket proclaiming allegiance to some American division during World War II.

"Did you get my message and is everything okay?" asked the swarthy man.

"Yes, everything is arranged. We wanted you to see the girl and approve. I think she will be first rate. We used her last year when you were away."

The girl in question was called from the next room. She was young, about 22 years old, with shiny dark hair hanging below her shoulders. Except that her eyes were heavily made up, there was nothing remarkable about her. Yet something held the viewer's attention. She wore a pantsuit and had an expensive shoulder bag.

"You have all the instructions?" the swarthy man asked, looking her over carefully. She smiled and nodded.

"Any questions?" he asked. She shook her head. "Can't you talk?" he turned to the others. "My God, she isn't dumb, is she?"

"In which language do you want me to speak?" the girl asked with slight derision. "I am fluent in seven, so just let me know your choice."

"I want to make sure you know what to do. There must be no slip up. This is an important run." The leader looked at the girl with greater interest. She was definitely attractive, he would get to know her later. But for now, business was business.

"Relax," she laughed easily. "I know what to do. I will go to the Taj Hotel and have a good time in Bombay. The rest will be taken care of. I've been on this run before. I know my way around."

"See that you do," he said, but softened the words with a smile. Yes, he would certainly like to know her a lot better when this job was over. As she was leaving he called after her. "What is your name?"

She gave him an amused, knowing look. "They usually call me Dolly," she drawled.

The man in the faded jeans was pleased to see the boss satisfied with their operator. He looked like a hippie but was actually a very wealthy man and high up in the organization. The next run would make them all richer, and he was relaxed and confident.

"By the way," he said, as he started to pour the red wine into the glasses, "we must arrange another passport. This one will have to be abandoned after the run is successful. What about the one you had in mind?" He handed the wine around.

The swarthy man stroked his small moustache. "I'm arranging that," he said. "You'll be informed in the usual way." Ignoring the glass of wine he nodded to the group and left the room. He walked down the street and turned onto a busy avenue. Here he hailed a taxi and gave his address. Once home, he went straight to the telephone and dialled a number.

"Hello chicken," he said, "missing me?"

"Oh, bunny hug," answered Sheela in delight. "Where have you been? I've been waiting for a call for *ages*. When are we going to meet?"

"What about tomorrow at the usual time?"

"Lovely," she answered and made kissing noises into the phone.

Her lover was certainly no Apollo – nothing to look at. Why was she so crazy about him? It's just one of those things, she thought, and turned her mind to tomorrow.

Meanwhile, Mona had been introducing Anil to her friends. She and Anil were enjoying being away from home where they both seemed constantly under Savitri's vigilance. They had been over to La Boutique where Anil had bought a few things to take home as gifts.

Gloria was intrigued by Anil and longing to ask Mona all about him but first she wanted to probe her about the scandalous talk going around about her boots being found in Jorge's bedroom!

"What's all this about your boots?" she asked, her eyes bright at the prospect of gossip – but she was disappointed with the reply.

Mona curtly answered that it was all rubbish.

Ignoring her, Francisca had taken Anil aside and said, "Something must be done about all this talk. It's crazy to pair that child's name with Jorge, especially now. The police will be snooping into every aspect of his life and jumping to conclusions. Please see if you can do something about it. Of course it's all nonsense, but people love to gossip."

"I'll do what I can," Anil assured her, but what on earth could he do? Francisca was relieved: Anil seemed such a steady young man.

Pepe joined them later in the day when they were having lunch at Chez Gourmet. It was a small French restaurant with a pavement café under a violet and white striped awning. Pepe came to their table as they sat looking at a menu printed in violet ink to match the awning.

"The quiche, my dears," he said. "It's the *specialité de la maison*." But he ordered an *omelette aux fines herbes* for himself. "My tummy is a bit queasy since that awful day," he confided. "I still can't decide whether or not I should go to the police. It is such a dreadful decision to have to make alone." He looked consideringly at Anil. "Perhaps I should talk to you instead."

"Please don't do that," Anil said, in alarm. "I'm a stranger here… all these foreign names are so confusing."

"But you have a sympathetic face, my dear. I can feel your aura of understanding. Yes, I think I will discuss the matter with you."

Mona smiled. People were always wanting to bring their problems to Anil. She had done it when she was a little girl and found herself doing it again. He really did have a sympathetic face and he really listened when you talked to him; not like those people who put on an expression of assumed interest while their minds wandered. Or was that only among diplomats, she mused.

"People always want to tell Anil their secrets," she told Pepe.

"It isn't a question of secrets at all," Pepe said huffily. "It's a matter of justice."

"Goodness," said Mona, surprised, "then by all means go to the police."

Pepe said goodbye to them both, adding "I shall call you, Anil, very soon and we shall talk about it. I must have the advice of a sympathetic soul. I am frantic with worry, my dear."

"Pepe is sweet, isn't he?" Mona asked Anil.

"He's nuts," was Anil's response.

Kwame was the most forthcoming of Mona's friends. He took Anil off on his own on a tour of the town and pointed out all the places of interest: the independence monument surrounded by flower beds, the national museum, a green wooded park named after the father of the nation. They ended up in his cubby-hole in the U.N. building.

"Something must be done to get Mona off the hook in this murder business," he said. "The kid's a nitwit to have lost her passport and left her boots at Jorge's and the police here love a scandal. Why doesn't her father fix things? In this country everything can be fixed."

"Sure, sure," said Anil, "in most countries things can be fixed one way or another. It's called 'dash' in yours, I believe!"

"Quite right. And in some places its called *mordida* and in others, 'B-and-C' for bribery and corruption. The point is that it exists everywhere. And Mona needs help that neither that cold fish of a father nor her mother can give her."

"Calm down. You're not giving her any help by all this running around behind the parents' backs. "

"Oh that!" Kwame threw back his head and had a good laugh. "It all started as a joke because I know what you Indians think of Africans."

"What do you mean?"

"Come off it. You people are the biggest racists going. I've heard plenty from friends who have lived in India – diplomats, students and so on. You fawn on Europeans and Americans and don't give a damn about anyone else." He laughed. "I heard a wonderful story from a chap from Accra who was studying in Delhi and was pretty homesick. He met some nice old girl, social worker or something, who asked him how he liked India. He told her it was fine, but he missed dates. Well, she was most upset that he hadn't had any and asked him over next evening and said he would most certainly have dates. When he got there, all worked up, she met him at the door with a big smile and a bowl of dates."

Anil burst out laughing. "Well, there it is," continued Kwame. "One gets culture shocks all the time. Mona is a good kid, too young for me, but she grows on you. Really, don't worry. We met at a diplomatic party and get together now and then because she doesn't have much fun at home. We are buddies, have coffee together, go to the movies, that's all."

Anil nodded. "I've known her since we were kids. Her Ma is planning a match between us. But to us it's a joke!"

"Well, Anil, I have to throw you out now," Kwame said at last. "Have to get back to the salt mines. Actually it's very interesting – I've been asked to find out something about a smuggling racket that has raised its ugly head recently."

"Take care," Anil said, thumping him on the back, leaving Kwame to his smugglers.

A little later, he met the Commissioner of Police leaving the embassy. He had come to the embassy for his interview with Mona wanting to be discreet; not wanting to cause the Ambassador the embarrassment of questioning her at police headquarters. He had heard her explanation regarding the mystery of the boots and reassured her parents that this was no incriminating evidence. He wanted to avoid all possible publicity of a scandalous nature, especially as diplomats were involved.

As Anil escorted him to his car, he said, "I feel for the Ambassador – a daughter is a great responsibility, and so young to be involved in a murder case. But we all know the Count was a charming man, very charming indeed." He gave Anil a man-of-the-world look. Anil was appalled.

"I assure you Commissioner," he began, but the Commissioner interrupted. "Poor little thing, in a strange land. In her country she would have been safe in a zenana."

"Believe me, sir," Anil insisted on having his say, "she probably has never heard the word. Things are very different nowadays..."

"I remember that wonderful old film," the Commissioner reminisced, "saw it on TV only the other night, *Moon over Bombay* or some such title. A beautiful maharani, young and in a zenana. Tyrone Power was the doctor, very handsome in Indian clothes. What an actor! You have a marvellous country, so spiritual! I would give anything to visit it, but I fear the terrible poverty would upset me too much. I cannot stand the idea of poverty. People dying of hunger, lying in the streets with no shelter. And all those sacred cows! No, unfortunately I can never go to India. I can't stand to see people suffer." And with a hearty handshake, the Commissioner finally stepped into his Cadillac and was driven away, leaving Anil with a bemused look on his face and a distinct feeling that he had lost his way in Wonderland.

FIVE

A Dinner Party

Bhagwan and Sheela were hosting a dinner for Anil. Sheela, who usually left the daily management of the house to Conchita because she could not be bothered, had taken pains to personally prepare a delicious Indian meal. She stood by the window enjoying that moment before the guests came, and feeling quite excited. She had had a fight with Bhagwan over the guest list but had managed to get her way. The French Counsellor and his chic wife were expected, as were the Indonesians and the Brazilians. A Mexican bachelor was bringing Gloria, Mona and Anil were coming, of course, and some others. They all arrived at more or less the same time. Drinks were passed by a waiter hired specially for the occasion and party sounds of ice tinkling in glasses, voices raised in chatter and laughter soon filled the room. In the background, Ravi Shankar's sitar could be heard on the tape recorder.

Anil stood with Bhagwan and a few guests in one corner of the room, all discussing the murder case and the lack of progress so far. Everyone wondered if the police had any clues. André, the Frenchman, said to Bhagwan, "I hope your chief is not too upset at all the gossip about Mona's boots."

"How do you know about the boots?" inquired Anil.

"In San Felice everything is known to everyone – they say

you dare not even dream without fear of your neighbours knowing what it's all about."

"A dangerous place!" laughed Anil.

"The Police Commissioner is a great admirer of your country, he is always talking about India," continued André. "I am sure he will be most discreet, especially with the international press."

"I hope so," Bhagwan said. He knew well that there was no truth in all the gossip about Mona and the Count.

"Well," Anil exclaimed, I don't know about the Commissioner's admiration for India but he told me the other day that he could never go there because he can't bear poverty."

"That's a good one: he has obviously not taken a tour of his own country. Plenty of have-not's right here," said André, smiling.

Bhagwan, who had been perfectly relaxed so far, was suddenly tense. His face flushed, breathing hard, he burst out "I can't stand such talk. Who do these people think they are, daring to criticize India and talk about poverty! The first time I met that Count chap, he was lounging in a chair with a crystal glass of champagne in one hand and a Romeo y Julieta cigar in the other. And he had the impertinence to say 'I fear my sensibilities would be lacerated at seeing starving people, that is the only reason I have never visited your beautiful country!' Can you imagine that? Lacerated, mind you, is the word he used! Does he think we are a country of starving beggars with some tigers roaming about here and there? I could have strangled him then and there!"

He stopped abruptly and there was a moment of embarrassed silence. Then, everyone started to talk at once. Bhagwan moved away to another group.

"What was he really like, this Count chap?" Anil asked André.

"Like any other rich playboy – richer than most and an Adonis to the ladies. He definitely had charisma. Here, they treated him like god. Like coffee, he was one of their main attractions, you understand."

"Any idea about the nature of the crime?" Anil wondered.

"It has no political undertones, which is surprising." André was thoughtful. "This is a very poor country you know; despite the millionaires, the ordinary people are very badly off. A revolutionary group bumping him off would have been understandable – or a kidnapping for ransom. But this..." he shrugged his shoulders. "Who can tell?"

After an excellent meal, followed by coffee and liqueurs, Anil found himself standing near Bhagwan again, and asked his host where he could get some reading matter on San Felice.

"There is a good public library but the books are in Spanish, of course. I have a fairly decent collection and you are welcome to take what you like, or come and browse here."

"I'd like that, thank you. But I'd prefer coming when you are home so we can have a chat." Anil had been a bit alarmed by Sheela's flirtatious ways. "What about Sunday?"

"Good. We'll have a beer and you can see if there is something to interest you among my books."

They wandered away and soon people began the preliminaries to leave-taking. One of the guests, a swarthy man with a small moustache who had been the life and soul of the party with his jokes and anecdotes, insisted the entire gathering move to his house for an after-party.

"The night is young," he kept saying, "What about coming over to my place? We'll open up some champagne and have one for the road."

Some of the guests demurred. Only Sheela was enthusiastic, exclaiming, "What fun! I adore impromptu suggestions!" But Bhagwan was adamant. "Tomorrow is a working day and it is late now."

"Who is that chap?" Anil asked Mona, as he drove her home. "I gather Bhagwan's not keen on him."

"Old Bhagwan is not keen on anything except work," replied Mona. "But that fellow is a bit odd. He goes everywhere and knows everyone and he hasn't even been to school. It's true – he boasts of it to me. 'Look where I've got without any schooling' is one of his favourite refrains."

"Where has he got?"

"Goodness knows, but he has a BMW and a Mercedes and a penthouse in New York and Meissen coffee cups, so it must be somewhere with lots of money." Mona yawned, tired. But she knew she would be awake once she was in bed. The passport had not turned up. There was no point searching for it anymore; she had been doing so over and over again. She wondered if it could have slipped out of her jacket pocket and fallen into one of her boots when she was pulling them off. That was a possibility. But then why had the police not found it there? Tomorrow she would have to tell her parents it was lost. The boots had been bad enough, with the yelling she had got from Mama and that awful old policeman with his mock-solicitous manner and his insinuating look. What would happen when she told her parents about the passport?

As soon as the last guest had left, Bhagwan shut the front door and locked it. The waiter had already left and no doubt Conchita had gone off leaving the kitchen full of dirty dishes.

"Why do you have to make such a tamasha about everything?" he asked Sheela, his face as grim as his voice. "Where was the question of going anywhere else at this time of the night? And with that man! My God, I don't know why I let you persuade me to invite him tonight. If you only knew what I do..." he stopped for a moment then continued, "I warn you, he is not ever to set foot in this house again".

"What do you know about him? You are the biggest spoilsport, that much *I* know about *you*. Where was the harm in going on, for a bit of a binge?"

"Understand me: he is not to come to this house again!"

"Oh, shut up!" Sheela left the room in a temper.

"If I knew what he knows indeed," she fumed as she went to her bedroom. "He'd certainly have a fit if he knew what I know!" Thinking about it put her in a better mood. She pulled off her exquisite sari – midnight blue woven with gold threads – and flung it on the ground with her blouse and underthings. Stretching luxuriously, she slipped on her nightie. Can't bother brushing my teeth, she thought, and slapping some cold cream on her face she got into bed. By the time Bhagwan came to their room, she was fast asleep.

No such escape awaited Bhagwan. He kept cursing himself for letting Sheela coax him into inviting that blackmailing scoundrel to his home. In the relief of Jorge's death he had given in to her request – of course she didn't really know the sort of man he was, how could she? And he was socially accepted everywhere. He had even been at that ill-fated party of Jorge's. God, what a mess he had made of everything: his marriage, his career. Marriage had been taken out of his hands by the family and the decision had been made by them. He had merely acquiesced. As a member of the foreign service he was considered a 'catch'. His colleagues used to say, "Don't fool around with Indian girls, they only want marriage." Well, why shouldn't they? It was a legitimate ambition and he was not one to fool around in any case. When a number of flattering proposals were received by his parents he realized that marriage was inevitable, and when he first met Sheela he thought she was shy and very sweet. Who could have thought she would be so totally changed in a few years? All she seemed to care about was her own pleasure. She was bold with men, flirting with all and sundry. Perhaps if there had been children... but why try to imagine a child in this home with a mother like Sheela and a father like – what was he? He dared not formulate any word. "I must ask the doctor for sleeping pills," he thought, "I can't go on like this." He finally got into his bed but the comfort of sleep eluded him.

"Mama," said Mona, "I have lost my passport."

"Nonsense, it can't be lost. Go at once to your room and look for it," replied her mother.

"I have looked everywhere, I know it's lost. I had it with me the day I went out riding with Jorge."

"What?" exclaimed Savitri. "And *today* you tell me! You don't even mention it to me for a whole week!" Her voice rose as she continued. "I hope you didn't leave it with your boots, otherwise the police will think you were planning to run away with Jorge or something stupid like that. Don't you know it is a very serious matter to lose your passport? Get out of this room before I lose my temper. Go and look for it at once. I have to do accounts with Gulati Singh." Turning from her daughter, she shouted for the cook.

Gulati came in furtively, reasonably clean for once and shaved. He had his account book in his hand and a blunt pencil behind one ear.

"Bibiji," he said, "I wish you would listen to me and make a *manat* to the Devi. If you like I will write home to my wife and she will go to our village priest and the matter will be taken care of. With police around and poor Jorge Sahib dead it is very important. We must prevent harm from coming to the house."

"Shut up you fool," snapped Savitri, and taking his account book she started to look through it. At the end of a long list of items was the note 'Due to Cook' against an astronomical figure. "Rubbish," said Savitri and put a thick line through it. "This is certainly not due to you."

"But Bibiji," began Gulati.

"Don't be more of a fool than you are," she shouted, and gave him the order for the day's meals. She handed him a few crumpled notes and left the room.

Gulati Singh stood for a minute, looking at the notes in his hand. Fewer than he expected to receive. True, he had padded the account a little, but then which cook doesn't, he thought. Anyway he had not stolen Bibiji's money. He had used it to buy a pair of earrings for Conchita. How happy she had been! Well, he would just have to think of some other way to make good the amount spent on those earrings. Bibiji was hard as a rock.

Later in the afternoon, Savitri sat behind a large tray pouring tea for Anil. It was Ram Nath's afternoon off and Gulati Singh had brought in the tea on a kitchen tray without the cloth meant to cover it. He shuffled in, a not very clean apron flung over his shoulder. As usual he had placed the teapot on the left side of the tray which made pouring awkward, and he had forgotten the milk strainer and a spoon for the sugar bowl. Savitri was furious with him – she rarely saw him without losing her temper – but she curbed herself for now because she had important matters to discuss with Anil and wanted Gulati Singh out of the room.

"Everything all right, Bibiji?" he remained where he was, beaming at Anil.

"Yes, Gulati, you may go."

"Shall I quickly make a few pakoras for the Sahib?"

"No, we don't want anything more. Go!"

At last, he ambled out. He knew why Anil was there and wanted very much to provide good things for him to eat. After all, he said to himself, he is going to be our son-in-law and we must see that everything is properly done while he is in the house.

Anil accepted a cup of tea from Savitri and took a cucumber sandwich from a platter near him.

"What nice little animals," he said, to distract Savitri's attention from Gulati Singh. He pointed to some ceramic figures displayed on a table.

"Yes, quite sweet. Mona made them in her class."

"She has talent," said Anil. Savitri looked at him with interest.

"Do you really think so?" she asked with a pleased smile. "She has given them all very odd names. The camel is Popocatapetl, the duck is Cotopaxi and that fat elephant is Chimborazo, I think. I wanted her to call that horse Aparajita – it has such an invincible look, doesn't it? But Mona downright refused. Said it wasn't a mare and she had named it Fuego after a volcano in Guatemala! I tried to tell her that if she must name things they should have nice Sanskrit names – after all we are Indians – but no, she will never pay attention to me."

"She is still very young," Anil knew where this conversation was leading and he wanted to avoid a confrontation with Aunty if possible. "By the way, I have had a word with the police and her boots will be returned in a day or so. The Commissioner asked me to tell you that they will not figure in any court proceeding."

"But what about all the talk?" fretted Savitri. "It makes me sick to think of Mona's name being bandied about like that. Sometimes I feel like slapping the girl for the foolish things she does."

Anil soothed her and finally she said, "Of course the child should be settled. And you too, Anil. It's high time you were thinking of getting married."

"Oh no, Aunty," said Anil, laughing. "That thought is very far from my mind. As for Mona, she really is too young. Give her time to grow up: she will have lots of suitors when you take her home."

"And what about that Black?" Savitri seethed with indignation.

"Oh Kwame! He is just a friend – no question of romance there. By the way he is a very nice fellow."

"A nice fellow indeed! You are all alike, you young people! Mixing with Hottentots and marrying out of India!"

"Now, Aunty," Anil was in a favourable position as far as Savitri was concerned and could speak his mind. "Kwame is not a Hottentot, as you well know, and what about people in your generation and even earlier who married the landlady's daughter while they were studying abroad? At least our generation choses its own intellectual level."

Savitri was not at all pleased by this kind of talk. What had happened to a proper sense of respect for elders?

"The way you young people talk is not right," she said. "Look at that Sheela. She had the impertinence to say once, and in front of foreigners, that she thinks marriage is all nonsense and everyone should be free to lead their own lives. And one day when I offered her some fresh orange juice she told me, bold as brass, that she only drinks passion-fruit juice! Some man who was present made a ribald remark and the girl laughed at it. I was stunned! I gave her a good scolding there and then, I can tell you." She paused for breath and then carried on. "In our young days we never dared to talk like that in front of the Ambassador's wife. And some that I knew were really terrible, making us do all kinds of things for them. I have never been like that, I'm like a mother to the whole staff. I try to help Sheela, but she has a reputation for being fast. Some people even say that Jorge was interested in her but that I don't believe for a moment. I'm sure Bhagwan must have heard that bit of gossip, poor man."

Anil changed the subject tactfully and they drank their tea. Savitri regretted all the diversions in their conversation, but she thought with satisfaction that at any rate the subject had been broached; men never thought of marriage until nudged to do so. Now she must allow some time for the seed to take root. After all, she had Anil's mother as an ally.

"Anil, is that you?"

"Yes, who is speaking?"

"My dear, it is I, Pepe. Can you pop over and have a drinkie with me at the Safari Club this evening?"

"Yes of course, Pepe. May I bring Mona?"

"Certainly not. I have to see you alone on a personal and very urgent matter. Come about six, then we'll be alone before the cocktail crowd comes in."

Anil was glad to leave the house. All that marriage talk from Aunty was rather unsettling. She never could take a hint, and he was prepared for several such harrowing sessions.

He got to the Safari Club soon after six and was immediately sucked into Darkest Africa. From every available space on the walls, trophy heads glared accusingly down at him. There were eland, bison, zebra, panther, lion and many other animals he could not immediately identify. Giant tropical plants grew in huge tubs. Crocodiles lay half-in, half-out of realistic jungle pools. Near the entrance a crouching jaguar, hidden by tall grasses, seemed to be waiting to attack the unsuspecting. In this artificial twilight, he saw Pepe beckon to him from one end of the long, empty bar.

"Good heavens, Pepe, why did you choose this place? I've been scared out of my wits ever since I entered the room."

"Rather good, isn't it? I find this place adorable. The trophies belong to a black sheep of an uncle of mine who used to go on a safari every year. He loved Africa. He gave me a darling elephant foot made into an umbrella stand. You'll see it when you come to my place. Anyway, he got into all kinds of trouble and had to leave the country. His things were all auctioned off. I must say this place is delightful."

"I didn't realize you were so bloodthirsty, Pepe!"

"It's the atmosphere, my dear. Slightly grotesque and quite fantastic."

They ordered their drinks. The barman put frosted tumblers in front of them and left them alone.

"Anil, I've asked you over because you are an outsider – the best person to advise me. You will be unbiased. With my other friends there is too much talk and no real understanding of the basic me, you understand? And of course one can't go to older people because they never do understand."

"What's the big mystery?" demanded Anil.

"Well, to put it bluntly, my dear, Jorge made me a certain proposal." Pepe looked sideways at Anil to gauge his reaction. "He wanted me to be his protégé. He wanted us to go away together on a trip. Well, naturally, I adored him. Everyone knows that. But I had to have a little time to think it over. I told him so. And the very next day he killed himself and I feel that I am his murderer."

"Are you mad?" Anil put his glass down with a bang and stared at Pepe. "I'm not concerned with your fantasies, but Jorge was stabbed, man, he did not commit suicide. Surely you know that?"

Pepe toyed with the silver buttons on his flowered waistcoat as he looked at Anil, quite calmly. He took a sip of sangria and said, "Yes, I know he was viciously stabbed, but I could be called his murderer."

"And what did you do with the weapon?"

"That is not the point," Pepe waved the matter away with one hand as he picked up his glass. "The point is that I am morally responsible. I am in torment and you must tell me where my duty lies."

"Your duty lies in shutting up," Anil said, brutally. "Don't talk such rot."

"Well if that is your attitude, my dear, there is not much point in discussing the matter further. You know, I was mistaken in you, Anil. I really sensed a sympathetic aura..." and with a graceful motion he slid off the bar stool and walked out of the room, leaving Anil to finish his drink alone and to settle the bill.

Returning to the embassy, Anil found Mona back from her class. She demanded to know where he had been, without her. He told her about the Safari Club and the shock it had been to his system. He added, "Pepe seems to think your handsome Count was in love with him."

"What!" Mona was aghast. "So such things do happen!"

"Well, surely you know the facts of life, Mona. With all this talk of gay liberation and so on you could hardly help knowing!" He was quite exasperated with her.

"Yes, but what do they do?" she wanted to know.

"Never mind and for God's sake stop pestering me!"

SIX

A Lacy Hanky

In the little beehive of the Indian Chancery, tranquil days followed one upon the other. The Chancery was located in a small house in a narrow street which had once been part of a good residential area. The house had been rented on a long lease in better days when the roads were less congested and the surrounding houses had been gracious private homes. But now the entire area was commercial and many homes were being pulled down to give way to multi-storeyed office buildings.

Inside the Chancery was a large entrance hall hung with colourful posters displaying the wonders of India. Indian newspapers and magazines covered the racks. On a large table, an Air India maharaja smiled beguilingly at visitors even though San Felice did not lie on the route of that airline. On one side of the hall was a reading room and library containing cupboards full of books, and pictures of Indian dignitaries hung on its walls. On the other side of the hall were small rooms devoted to the consular office and the sanctum sanctorum of the cipher clerk. Upstairs, the Ambassador reigned supreme in his big sunny office, with his other officers and secretaries at hand nearby. Everyone was busy with their duties but the truth was that nothing much really happened here. San Felice was half a world away from India and the average citizen of each country was blissfully unaware of the other.

Breaking the comfortable peace of the coffee hour came a call from the Ambassador, informing his consular officer that his daughter's passport had been lost. It created a mild mid-morning stir. "That girl should be in college in India instead of learning to make pots and pans here."

"It's not a bad hobby and she can earn some pocket money doing ceramics after she is married."

"What? In India, where every villager makes better pots than hers?"

"Of course, the parents should arrange a good match for her... not as if she is pretty... dark too..."

"Who knows, perhaps this Mr Anil, he seems like a steady young man..." And so they drank their coffee and wondered where the passport could be, and how it had come to be lost.

"I'll have to inform all missions about this," said the consular officer as he left the room. He was a tall young Sikh who drew many interested comments in San Felice with his turban of different hues. Today he was wearing one of salmon pink. The girls found him attractive but Balbir Singh was a modest young man and his social life revolved around the embassy families. The wives of his colleagues treated him like a younger brother and cooked his favourite food when he visited for Sunday lunch.

Balbir left the office as it was his day to go to the airport to receive the incoming weekly bag from Delhi. The airport was a small one compared with modern international airports but several airlines passed through it and it had a pleasant shopping area with the usual duty-free shops as well as a few booths selling local handicrafts. Passengers awaiting flights shopped at the booths or drank the excellent local coffee. Balbir, having to wait for a bit for his plane to arrive, sat down and had his shoes polished by a small shoeshine boy. As an outgoing flight was announced, a stream of passengers walked past Balbir towards the gate for security checks. His shoes shined, he stood up and watched them hurry by. Among them was a young girl with neat black hair coiled in a bun, wearing jeans and high-heeled shoes and carrying an expensive shoulder bag. Balbir had never heard of Dior, but as she went past him he caught a whiff of a heady perfume. Nearing the queue waiting at the security gate, the girl opened her bag to take something out. A tiny handkerchief appeared and, unnoticed by her, fell to the ground. Hardly knowing what he was doing, Balbir walked towards it and picked it up to return to the girl. Meanwhile, she had moved on and the line had been joined by a family with several children. He hesitated and once more the intoxicating fragrance came to him, making his senses reel. Without thinking what he was doing, he put the scrap of lacy cloth into his pocket. He turned for another look at the girl and thought vaguely that she reminded him of someone. Then he returned to his chair to wait for his plane and in half an hour had collected the bag and returned to the chancery. But somehow the girl from the airport kept coming into his thoughts, even as the heady scent of the handkerchief disturbed him from working on his file. Who was she and why did he keep thinking of her?

Anil walked over to the Narains' house for his morning date with Bhagwan. His host was pottering around the garden aimlessly and called out a welcome.

"I didn't know you were a garden person," remarked Anil.

"Don't know one plant from another," said Bhagwan. "I just like to get out of the house. These days I'm not sleeping well and everything gets on my nerves."

"Well, the house I have just left is in a state of feverish activity, to say nothing of utter chaos. They are preparing for Republic Day with a vengeance – I'm glad to be out of it."

"I can imagine. Let me guess – Madam yelling, Mona cowering and H.E. locked up in his study!"

"Bull's-eye," said Anil laughing. "H.E. really loves his study. Last night he condescended to ask me in for a nightcap. He has a bottle hidden behind some volumes on finance. Says they are so dull nobody will remove them! And while I was his captive, he gave me a lecture on his daggers – quite a collection but I don't think any are genuine antiques. I wonder why he keeps them."

"Maybe to murder his wife. She's a most irritating woman."

"You know, Bhagwan, you should be careful what you say, even as a joke. With police all over the place questioning people, you could give the wrong impression."

"My God!" Bhagwan burst out laughing and was still guffawing when Sheela came out to join them a little later.

"What's the joke? Hi, Anil," she said. "We are going off to the seaside for a weekend soon, like to come along? It's just a couple of hours drive and there's a lovely beach."

"I forgot to tell you," Bhagwan said sobering up. "We've been asked by some friends and I'm looking forward to sleeping in the sun on the beach."

"And it's a duty-free port," Sheela chimed in, "so I'm looking forward to lots of shopping while Bhagwan sleeps. You really should come with us. Our friends have a big sprawling house and they won't mind a bit."

"Sounds good, but I can't do that. I should be planning my departure but H.E. and Aunty won't hear of it."

"I'll bet." Sheela looked amused.

"No, it's not because of Mona, though the old girl has cornered me a few times on the subject of marriage. She really is very worked up over the police investigation. She even asked me the other day if I didn't think a stain on one of the daggers looked like blood. Of course it was no such thing but at one point she was all for getting it tested. Can you beat that?"

"She's nuts," said Bhagwan. "Look here, Anil, what exactly did she say about the blood stain?"

"Oh, nothing special and she just went on and on – you know how she is when she gets something in her head."

"Yes, one stops listening," Bhagwan said. Then he turned to Anil and said, "Look, if you'd like to come over while we are away, do so, and help yourself to books. That maid of ours is supposed to be on duty all the time we are away. I hope she will not be over too often at the embassy kitchen with that fool of a cook. Anyway we'll meet before that at the party on Republic Day – we can't go until that is over." He walked Anil to the gate in silence. Suddenly he seemed to be somewhere else.

"I wonder what's biting him," Anil thought, as he turned round to wave goodbye and saw Bhagwan standing there, a vacant look on his face. Anil could not understand this sudden change of mood, but supposed that Bhagwan had office matters on his mind.

The police, meanwhile, had not been inactive. Under the direction of the Commissioner himself, they had questioned and fingerprinted a large number of people: the minions who had cleaned, cooked, served and provided the music for the Count's last party. The Commissioner had not deemed it suitable for the elite who attended the function to be fingerprinted. After all, many were well known to him personally, friends of a lifetime, and therefore not to be thought of as suspects. Others had been diplomats and he had no desire to create a diplomatic incident. However, a certain amount of discreet questioning could not be avoided and this had been carried out. It had been a thankless task with not a single clue coming to light, despite the best efforts of his most reliable officers. Only one bizarre incident was reported, but when the Commissioner was informed of it he shrugged it off impatiently.

This incident was related to a visit made by a police officer to the apartment building in which Pepe resided. On the day of his visit the officer went up to the fourth floor where he was admitted into a very well-furnished apartment. He looked around the small living room with appreciation while the valet-butler went to inform his master of the visit. There were a great many fine paintings and bibelots in the room and the furnishings were mushroom-coloured curtains, cream-coloured upholstery and a large old Persian carpet. One item was thoroughly out of place, however, in that elegant room: a hideous elephant foot made into an umbrella stand. The police officer had been disturbed at the sight.

From behind the closed door of what he supposed must be the bedroom, came the sounds of Vivaldi's 'Four Seasons'. Suddenly the music stopped, in the middle of the winter sequence; the door flew open and framed in it stood an exquisite being, not quite of this world. Pepe's face was becomingly flushed and his long, honey-coloured hair was in considerable disarray. He wore flared trousers of a rich burgundy colour and his ruffled shirt front was not quite buttoned. He threw out his arms and exclaimed in a high voice, "So you have come at last! Arrest me! Where are the handcuffs? What are you waiting for? I am a murderer and I deserve punishment. I have been waiting and waiting for you to come and at last you are here. Arrest me and end this farce!"

The police officer looked blank, as he marvelled at this quite unusual sight. *Caramba*, am I dreaming? he thought. When he was able to collect his wits, he stammered that he had come for a routine check and had no warrant for an arrest. But Pepe was so vehement that he began to wonder if, after all, there might be something in what this beautiful young man claimed. If so, he should make an immediate report to his superior officer. Excusing himself excitedly, he practically ran out of the room and drove straight to police headquarters where he made a full and somewhat dramatic report.

Nothing came of it, however, as Pepe's grandfather was a Very Important Person. Moreover the valet-butler and the doorman of the apartment building vouched for the fact that Pepe had returned from the party no later than 1:25am and had gone straight to bed in a state of mild inebriation. Added to this was the testimony of the Count's superior butler, who had been in the family for thirty years and was the brother-in-law of Pepe's mother's cook; he said that it was common knowledge that Pepe could not stand the sight of blood.

SEVEN

National Day Reception

Republic Day dawned bright and sunny as always, as was customary at this time of the year in San Felice. The reception was a noon one, from 12 to 2pm, and Savitri's shouting and screaming, all directed at the servants, had borne fruit. The house looked positively radiant. The parquet floors were slippery enough to be dangerous and each piece of silver or brass gleamed with polish. Huge floral arrangements dotted the hall and reception rooms giving the place, according to Mona, the look of a funeral parlour. In the garden a few striped umbrellas and cane furniture provided shade and rest. The large herbaceous border was looking its best and the camellia shrubs had burst into flower a few days ago, as if they knew that they were expected to be at their finest. On the verandah too, pots of fuchsia bloomed profusely. It was a pretty sight and one that gladdened Savitri's heart. She had worked hard and now she saw perfection.

She stood at her husband's side and, next to them, the visiting delegation made a long receiving line. The Ambassador was formally dressed in the black achkan and tight trousers of his national costume. Savitri, too, was in full regalia – including her special party smile – in a deep purple sari with a broad gold border, heavy gold ornaments encircling her neck and wrists and hanging from her ears. Earlier she had been furious with Mona, who had appeared for the party dressed simply in a light pink chiffon sari and no ornaments. "Child, you are trying my patience!" she had ranted, in a temper. "Go at once and change into the sari I chose for you and put on the jewellery I put out on your dressing table. Here I am all dressed up for a big occasion and you come out in this old rag. A young girl should always be in bright clothes. And don't forget to put something around your neck!"

"But Mama, how can I wear all that gold in the afternoon? And it's so hot in the garden."

"Stop arguing and go at once. The guests will soon be here."

So Mona had gone reluctantly and after sulking briefly, she had given in to the inevitable and done as she was told. Now she stood in the garden, looking miserable and dressed as if for a formal ball in a turquoise sari embroidered all over with gold peacocks. She was not looking forward to the party though some of her friends had been invited. Not Kwame, though. At the suggestion, Mama had looked as if she would have an apoplectic fit and Anil had advised her not to bring up controversial subjects at a time when her mother was under pressure.

Before long, a stream of cars started to drive past the tulip trees and turn in at the gate of the embassy. Guests began to file past the receiving line and into the garden. They included several officials of the San Felice government, including the Commissioner of Police, members of the diplomatic corps, the elite social set and the less elite but more interesting friends of the embassy staff. The Bharatiya Samaj of San Felice was there in full force with its two non-diplomatic members – a young Indian who taught sitar and an elderly gentleman with an untidy beard and a muffler round his head, who had come some years ago to preach a religion he said he had invented, one of peace and brotherly love.

The garden gradually filled with people and white-coated waiters glided to and fro with trays full of spicy snacks and icy glasses of coloured drinks.

"Have you tried these delicious samosas?" one guest said to another. "They are scrumptious!"

"What is this, an Indian chutney?" asked a lady, helping herself to a corn chip with cheese dip.

"These little meatballs are too, too divine. I'm going to forget all about my diet for today," said one plump lady to her companion.

The foreign women in their airy cottons admired the brilliant colours and the handwoven silks of the Indians and embarked on an inquisition about this marvellous native dress: how many meters of cloth were there in a sari? how did one put it on? how did it stay on once it was put? They exclaimed over and over what a perfectly flattering dress a sari was for Indian women and how it put European women at such a disadvantage. The embassy wives, dressed in their best, stood in a group while all this talk went on, looking pleased and self-conscious.

The visiting members of parliament and others of the delegation were finally released from the receiving line and began to mingle with the guests. Their dress proclaimed that they belonged to various parts of the country and different social groups. There was one gentleman in a snowy lungi who was obviously from southern India, a gold-bordered angavastra over his shoulders. Another wore crumpled loose pyjamas with a tweed achkan open at the neck. Two men were dapper in western clothes. One of the women wore a lovely sari shot with crimson threads but spoiled the effect with the tennis shoes she had strangely chosen to wear with it.

A harassed Second Secretary went up to one of the MPs who was wearing a neat dhoti and kurta and asked if he could fetch a drink for him.

"I don't drink."

"No alcohol is served, sir, there are only soft drinks."

"Oh well, in that case I'll take a small juice." He spoke in a tone of resignation. He had spent many years working with landless peasants and had the brave look of one who expects the worst and is seldom disappointed.

The secretary rushed off to find a waiter and nearly collided with two visiting women who were having an animated talk with Sheela. He heard one ask, "Does the Ambassador's wife do any social work?" but could not wait for Sheela's answer.

On the other side of the lawn, a middle-aged parliamentarian who had been quite a lad in his youth, had discovered Mona and piloted her towards the blooming camellias. As a waiter passed by, he helped himself to a tomato juice off the tray and gave Mona a wink.

"With a little forethought one can manage to have a bloody mary even on a dry day," he said and before her astonished gaze he produced a hip flask and poured a stream of vodka into his tomato juice. "Care for some?" he asked.

"Oh no," replied Mona, quite shocked. "I don't drink alcohol."

"That's odd. I thought all you young people who live abroad drink and take drugs."

"Well, some do, most don't," said Mona trying to avoid the persistent hand that lingered on her arm.

"Oh, come come, my dear, that's a very ambiguous remark," said the MP, pinching her cheek.

"I think I must go and see if my mother needs me," Mona said desperately.

"Don't stay away too long," said her companion, with a roguish look. After a final squeeze he let her go and moved to a group nearby, sipping his tomato juice thoughtfully. Mona made her escape, with relief.

The peak of the party arrived; voices raised in loud chatter and waiters weaving in and out of the crowd bearing their trays of refreshment. In the kitchen, Gulati Singh was in seventh heaven. All the hard work of preparation was worth the trouble because his food was much appreciated. Not much was left, and a few guests had even found their way into the kitchen and helped themselves to snacks straight from the source. One had even asked how those delicious stuffed triangles were made.

"And you know, Conchita," he said to the Narains' maid who had come over to help with the washing up. "I saw, with my own eyes, one lady put two samosas in a paper napkin and tuck them into her bag." For him this was high praise.

I must remember to tell Bibiji, he thought.

Finally the guests started to leave, and soon the lawn was nearly empty. It looked like a deserted battlefield, full of holes made by the women's high-heeled shoes, cigarette stubs, crumpled paper napkins here and there and bits of fallen food. Only the Indian community was left and Savitri called loudly to invite everyone to come into the house to rest and to have a little of what she called "pot luck."

"Well, that was an excellent party," said one of the MPs. Of the entire group that came wearily into the house, he was the only one in good spirits due to the vodka in his tomato juice. All the others looked worn out from the torture of standing for hours and making conversation with people they did not know.

"National Day parties are going out of style," the Ambassador remarked. "Many countries don't have them anymore for one reason or another and I must say they are generally a waste of time. One can make better contacts over a dinner than at a huge reception."

"That's a very strange remark," said the woman in tennis shoes who had wanted to know about Savitri's social work. "I think it is essential to have a reception to mark a special day and to show foreigners that we glory in the day we became a Republic." She looked most belligerent.

"I agree with you entirely," said the Ambassador smoothly. "That is why we had the reception today, and also to introduce you to San Felice. Your presence here was responsible for this good attendance."

Savitri noticed that the jovial MP had his arm around Mona and she called to the girl to go and see what was going on in the kitchen. Then she beckoned to Ram Nath to bring out more fruit juice.

"Do let me give you some of my concoction," she said with a smile to the angry lady. She did not want any breakages like that glass table-top in Syria. "This is papaya with watermelon and orange, my own recipe. It is really delicious." She handed glasses around. "No, no, Sheela, not for you. I have got passion-fruit juice especially for you," she added, making a show of handing a glass of the fragrant nectar to Sheela – who took it with a toss of her head, saying it was her favourite. Savitri looked at Bhagwan and saw him stiffen.

Lunch was announced and Savitri urged the guests to make their way into the dining room and have a little something to eat. Guests were greeted by a large buffet of several appetizing dishes, including pickles and breads, fruit and desserts. Despite their fatigue and the generous amount of snacks served in the garden, most people made a good meal. Savitri, like a traditional Indian hostess, urged more and more on the visitors. To those who declined another helping she said, with an arch look, "Ah, I see you are dieting," and continued to press them to eat more. Everyone seemed quite happy with the sumptuous Indian spread. One gentleman, however, was heard telling one of the embassy staff members that it was remarkable how well Indians on duty abroad managed to live and eat. He pointed out, for instance, that at home putting almonds in a chicken dish was not to be thought of; almonds were far too expensive in India. The recipient of this information, Hidayat Khan, was quite upset as he was the embassy accountant and wondered if he should inform the Ambassador later that foreign allowances might well be trimmed as a result of Gulati Singh's good cooking.

Coffee was served on the verandah afterwards and Anil and Bhagwan helped Ram Nath to pass around the cups. There seemed to be one or two cups short, and Bhagwan begged Savitri to take his. "I think I'll pass it up," he told her. "It seems to keep me awake at night even if I take it at lunch." Savitri, who was tired after the long afternoon, took the coffee gratefully and drank it in gulps.

At long last, replete and sleepy, the guests rose to leave. The Ambassador looked around for his wife and noticed that she was absent. She had probably gone to give some instruction to the servants. He whispered to Mona to go and tell her mother that the guests were getting ready to leave and Mona slipped away, thankful to get away from the lavish compliments her elderly new admirer was paying her.

Suddenly there was a scream, and Mona came running back to the verandah.

"Papa, Papa!" she cried in fright. "Come quickly, something terrible has happened to Mama. She's fainted... she's ill..."

The Ambassador stopped for a minute to stare at Mona and then hurried with her into the house. Everyone rushed in behind the father and daughter and crowded around the figure of Savitri, lying in a huddle, on the ground near the kitchen. She was breathing stentoriously.

"Bhagwan – get a doctor quick! Take my car and fetch him." The Ambassador knelt by Savitri, taking her pulse. His face was white. Mona bent over her mother, crying. Anil tried to make people move back so that Savitri could have some air. But nothing was of any use; by the time the doctor arrived, Savitri was gone.

EIGHT

Aftermath of Tragedy

The sudden tragedy left everyone bewildered. What had happened? How could a happy, well-organized function end like this? It was a ghastly joke in bad taste. Tragedy had struck in such an odd, grotesque manner that nobody could quite accept what had happened.

The doctor had to give Mona a sedative and the women of the embassy managed, at last, to get her to bed. Very subdued, the other guests had left the house. Finally alone, the Ambassador took the doctor to his study and had a long private talk with him. It was revealed that Savitri had had a bad heart and had been under the doctor's care for some months.

"Savitri with a bad heart? I don't believe it. She was in perfect health, did yoga exercises every morning, never smoked or drank in her life." The ambassador shook his head in vehement disbelief. "How could this happen?"

"And yet she had been my patient…" the doctor reiterated.

"I knew she had consulted you but I thought it was for her digestion – she always had some problems with indigestion."

"No," the doctor insisted. "I was treating her for heart complaint. Perhaps the exertion of such a big party brought on a heart attack and…"

"Impossible. My wife was always arranging big parties or busy with other things. She was a very active woman, very active indeed. I just can't take this in."

"With a heart condition one never knows. Perhaps an autopsy to satisfy you?"

But the Ambassador was adamant. There must be no autopsy. If the doctor was satisfied, he was the best judge of the matter. The doctor finally left the house with suitable expressions of sympathy, but looking very grave and not happy with the manner of this death.

The next few days were somber. The Ambassador, with admirable control over his emotions, made all the necessary arrangements for the funeral, Bhagwan always at his side. When the sad event was over, Anil went to his host and suggested that he should move into a hotel before booking his ticket for the return journey to India. But the Ambassador would not hear of it.

"Nonsense, my boy. You must stay here a little longer and help us through these sad times. Mona needs you and so do I. Don't think of leaving yet."

Seeing the Ambassador's self-control, Anil doubted if he could be of any help to him – but Mona's pale face haunted him and he agreed to stay on for as long as he was needed.

With time on his hands, he had done a lot of reading and he decided to go over to Bhagwan's place to borrow some more books. He walked over and was nearly at the house when he remembered that the Narains would not be at home. They had at last been able to take the weekend off to visit their friend at the seaside. The Ambassador had urged them to do so.

As he was already on the threshold, Anil rang the bell and a dishevelled Conchita opened the door. She led him into the small den where Bhagwan kept his books. Anil put down the pile of books he was returning and stood looking at the titles of the ones on the shelves. Just then the phone began to ring and he picked it up on the fifth ring as Conchita had disappeared.

"Hello?" he inquired. There was silence at the other end. "Hello?" Again silence, except for a distant sound of breathing. Anil was puzzled and put the receiver down. He picked up a book at random and opened it. A sheet of paper fluttered down to the ground and as he retrieved it he could not help reading the message written on it, in childish capitals: YOUR WIFE IS CARRYING ON WITH YOU KNOW WHO DO YOU WANT IT KNOWN OR WILL YOU NOW DO AS I SAY.

With a look of distaste, Anil put the piece of paper back in the book and returned the volume to the shelf. Christ, he thought, poor old Bhagwan is being blackmailed, but why and by whom? Sheela could well be "carrying on" with someone. No wonder old Bhagwan looked so dismal and worn out most of the time. He was a heavy, slow chap and had always reminded Anil of a brontosaurus or another one of those lumbering dinosaurs. Now, he felt sorry for him. He decided to get away from this unhappy house. He was not fanciful by any means, but the atmosphere was getting to him. He decided to go and visit Kwame.

Kwame was sitting at an untidy desk with piles of papers all over the place when Anil arrived at his nearby office. He was pleased to see Anil and asked after Mona.

"I wrote to her after her mother's death but I would like to see her. I'm worried about the kid."

"She is in rather a bad way," Anil told him. "She has taken this tragedy very hard you know, and is in bed most of the time. I don't think she has even seen your letter. I'm worried about her too because it's not only grief: I feel she is full of remorse, as if she feels guilty about something."

"Well, you know how things were between her and her mother. It's natural for her to feel pretty bad about it now," Kwame said, gently.

But Anil shook his head. "It's more than that. I can't explain it but I feel quite anxious. She doesn't eat or talk... well, never mind all that. Tell me how your work is coming along."

Kwame brightened and cleared his desk the easy way, pushing all the papers to one side. A whole heap fell on the floor and, laughing, he let them lie there.

"Remember I told you about that international gang? The inquiry is coming along well and it seems to be much bigger than we had imagined at first. Diamonds, we think."

"Diamonds!" Anil was interested. "Sounds like this has the makings of a mystery story. Anyway I thought smuggling these days involved cocaine and heroin and things like that."

"Drugs may be part of the game too. I just don't know. Actually I don't have the whole picture yet. They just got me into this for some journalistic type sleuthing."

"Speaking of sleuthing, I'm going to see the Police Commissioner to find out what's happening in the murder case. The old boy has taken a fancy to me and I want to make sure that Mona's name is definitely out of the police files."

"Let's go round to the corner place first," Kwame said. "It's time for a cup of good coffee."

The "corner place" he spoke of was a tiny coffee bar in which the smell of spaghetti seeped in from the Café Roma next door. They chose their table and gave the order to a young, bored-looking waitress.

The room was empty except for a table behind them where two men sat drinking coffee and talking in whispers. But then they began to speak in loud voices all of a sudden, appearing as if they were trying to attract the attention of Kwame and Anil. The words "Indian embassy" and "Indian Ambassador" kept recurring and looks were thrown at the other table.

Kwame looked at Anil and raised his eyebrows. Anil turned his chair around and stared at the speaker; it was impossible to ignore this kind of provocation. He saw a stout man in his early thirties, flamboyantly dressed in a loud, checked suit. As he waved his hand around, a heavy gold signet ring, set with a flashy stone, caught the light. His companion, a younger man, sat listening quietly.

"If you wish to contact the Indian Embassy I can give you the address," Anil said, addressing his voluble neighbour.

"No sir, very kind of you." The man smiled broadly, flashing a few gleaming gold teeth. "I know the place. It is some senior and responsible person I wish to see."

"I don't belong to the embassy so I can't help you." With that, Anil turned his chair around to face Kwame again.

"But I understand, sir, that you are a guest of the Indian Ambassador?"

"Good God!" Anil was amazed. "How do you know that? Who are you?"

"My name you would not know. Call me Gonzalez," answered the man, getting up and bowing in an obsequious manner. "Actually it is my mother's name. Perhaps you would be so kind as to spare me some time?"

"What for?" asked Anil rudely, staring at him.

"As I stated before, sir, the matter is confidential."

Kwame was intrigued. "I'll be off," he told Anil, giving him a look that urged him to get to the bottom of this matter, and before the other could object, he had gulped down his coffee and left. Gonzalez's friend had also disappeared quietly, and he approached Anil's table on his own.

"If you permit, sir?" he inquired, with an ingratiating smile.

"All right, sit down. What do you want?" demanded Anil.

"In case the Ambassador is interested, I have very confidential information for him. If you would be a, how do you call it, a go-between, perhaps a meeting could be arranged? It would be of advantage to both parties, I assure you."

"But what is all this about?" Anil insisted on some facts, but Gonzalez shook his head and smiled.

"I can only promise you that the matter is of real interest. Among other subjects I would like to speak of, there is the matter of the passport of His Excellency's daughter." He refused to say anything further or to go into any detail.

"*Hasta luego*," he said. Bowing again to Anil, he gave him a card with a telephone number written on it.

What the devil? thought Anil.

He was quite put off. He had come to San Felice for a little holiday and from the first moment he had found himself mixed up with a murder investigation then a sudden death. He was expected to be the confidant of nearly everyone he had been introduced to – and now was being contacted by doubtful characters in a sleazy cafe. It was a bit much. He had no intention of solving mysteries. Even though he was the author of a detective story, he did not wish to get involved in mysterious puzzles in a foreign country. He decided to get away from San Felice as soon as possible and, ignoring Gonzalez, left the restaurant in a disgruntled mood.

Walking down the street looking for a taxi stand, he passed a large poster announcing that *Young Frankenstein* was showing at a down-at-heel movie hall. It reminded him of his school days in Nainital, back in India, when he and his pals had stood in line on a Saturday afternoon to see some horror film at just such a dilapidated cinema hall. He put Gonzalez out of his mind, and with a smile, bought a ticket and went in.

The Ambassador sat in an easy chair in his study with a glass of his favourite whiskey in hand. He no longer had to hide the scotch; Ram Nath had brought in a cut-glass decanter of Highland Cream with a siphon and ice on a silver tray and left it on the table. Shocked as the Ambassador had been – and still was – at the wholly unexpected death of his wife, he felt that life had to go on. The stream of callers who had come to offer their condolences after this tragic event had been struck by his calm attitude. He had shown the right degree of grief – not too much to embarrass his friends but just enough to make them sympathize most sincerely with the widower left bereaved with an overwrought teenage daughter to care for and console.

He sat, thinking about the future. Ever since he had married, his life had been controlled by Savitri. In fact, to an extent that had been irksome to him. At times he had felt like a pampered dog; always taken for a walk on a leash but never allowed to scamper off and have fun on its own. But he was the kind of man who had as his motto 'anything for a quiet life' and he had put up with a good deal.

Without Savitri's managing hand, of course, the household was in a state of chaos. Gulati Singh, that perennial adolescent who was a fool but an excellent cook, and on whom Savitri used to daily vent her wrath, had broken down with grief at the death of his mistress. He had taken to his room and his mourning wails could be heard for several days and were most annoying. He kept sending messages through the other servants that if only a *manat* had been kept as he had begged many times, this catastrophe would not have befallen the family. Ram Nath had taken charge of the kitchen and unless some change occurred everyone would fall ill with dire stomach ailments. The only edible food the man could cook was scrambled eggs and there was a limit to how many times a day – and for how long – the family could submit to this limited diet. An excellent butler, but he had failed miserably as a cook.

And his daughter Mona, who had appeared to be at daggers drawn with her mother, had collapsed and though he understood her heartache, she could not be kept under sedation permanently. Even the doctor was getting anxious.

Sipping his whiskey, the Ambassador came to the conclusion that drastic changes would have to be made and fairly soon. It was high time anyway for him to think of his future. He was fifty years old and in a few years he would be on the retirement list. What had his life amounted to? He had to face the fact that in terms of his personal life, he had been little more than a henpecked husband. In his career, also, he had been second best. While colleagues no better or brighter graced European capitals or missions of great importance to India, he had been pushed around to what he considered second-class embassies. What was San Felice when all was said and done? No. He was determined to make a last effort. Too long had he allowed Savitri to manage things for him – though he had to give her credit for the excellent connections she had acquired in the relations of his daughters-in-law. He had already made tentative proposals for a job which would not only be better paid by far than his present one, but would give him great satisfaction as well.

"I'll show them," he thought. "I've got a few irons in the fire." He finished his drink and decided to go to bed and read. He had acquired some catalogues which would make pleasant reading until he felt sleepy.

Sheela was in an unusual state of turmoil. She had had a meeting with her lover and things had not been as peachy as always. To begin with, he had seemed angry that she and Bhagwan had gone out of town and he had not known about it. "Why didn't you tell me?" he kept asking her. And his insistence somehow had nothing to do with his wanting to be with her. "I called," he kept saying, "and some strange man answered." Of course they had made love and all that, but she had felt that something was wrong. When she was getting ready to leave he had made a most extraordinary request. Even now she could not believe it.

"Chicken, I want you to do something for me. Will you do me a favour?" She had looked at him expectantly and was surprised to hear him continue, "Can you let me have your passport for a few days?"

"My passport?"

"Just for a couple of days, chicken."

"But sweetie, I don't have my passport. It's kept in the office. And what in the world can you want it for?"

"Well, chicken, it's a bit tricky. I hate to ask but it would help me a lot if I could have a diplomatic passport to get a few things I have ordered. You know what customs are like here. It's a question of a small deal actually that I've made with a man I know in New York. I arranged it because I never thought you'd mind doing me a small favour."

What on earth was he talking about? What deal? Sheela could not make head nor tail of his words. Her passport was hers, with her picture in it; what good would a woman's passport be to him? She asked the question and his reply confused her even further.

"I thought I'd send my secretary over to collect the things. You know, along with the other stuff I have ordered a crystal set and a surprise for your pretty ears. I love them." He started kissing them, holding her close to him. She had wanted to ask him outright exactly what was behind this strange request but some instinct warned her against doing so, and instead she smiled in a babyish way, and said, "Sweetie, when you asked for a favour I thought you wanted to run away with your chicken!"

For a second she saw an impatient look, unlike his customary melting glance, flick across his face. Then it was gone. He pulled her to him and started to kiss her again and she was surprised to find that she could not respond.

Home at last, Sheela had tried to work the thing out. The only reason anyone not entitled to a diplomatic passport would want one was for an illegal purpose. That was clear. But what purpose? Espionage? Or, good grief, was he a cocaine lord or some such dreadful thing? He was very wealthy she knew, but had never bothered much with the nature of his work. Drugs and smuggling and things like that belonged to a make-believe world, the world of movies and novels. They had nothing to do with people one knew. Obviously she could not give him her passport and that nonsense about the surprise earrings was silly. How could she ever wear expensive jewels in her ears, and they must be jewels otherwise why the hoo-ha about customs? Bhagwan would notice immediately and ask where she had got them.

She had dived headlong into a love affair because of boredom at home and because she had been so assiduously courted. It had been carefree and frothy, with the added excitement of secrecy; she had openly had fun and flirted with lots of men but nobody had suspected that she had a lover. But now she felt betrayed and there was a hard lump in her middle. She had been made a fool of. Chicken indeed! And why had he been so put out to find she had gone out of town? With all the dreadful aftermath of Savitri's death, she had never even thought of calling him. Supposing he was a spy? The papers were always uncovering spy rackets among diplomats and in government circles. But why would a spy need a passport? A coded telegram would be another matter, but in that case the person to make love to would be the wife of the cipher clerk. At the thought of that placid lady, the mother of five, frolicking in bed with a spy, Sheela burst out laughing.

NINE

Police Visit Again

It was mid-morning and once more the Police Commissioner was in the office of the Ambassador.

"It is really a coincidence," he remarked, "that your daughter should have lost her passport at just this moment. Our sources inform us that the smuggling racket I was mentioning just now has been making use of diplomatic passports."

The Ambassador was not perturbed. He had informed his Counsellor as well as his consular officer about the loss of the passport immediately, and all precautions had been taken that very day. There was no problem there, he was sure. However, upon the Commissioner's insistence he sent for Balbir Singh. The young man entered the room, impeccably dressed as always, his lavender turban freshly starched. He gave an account of all the steps he had taken in connection with the loss of the passport.

"Send one more telex," said the Ambassador, and as Balbir pulled a small pad out of his pocket to take down the message, a scrap of lace came with it and fluttered unheeded to the floor. The slightly stale but recognizable fragrance that came from it made the Commissioner, a ladies' man, look at it with interest. He bent down to pick it up and shaking the lace hanky said, "Ah, Diorissimo!"

He glanced with interest at Balbir as he held the hanky

to his nose. "My congratulations, young man, on your *novia*'s taste."

Balbir blushed hotly. The Ambassador looked up at him sharply, and then at the handkerchief in the Commissioner's hand. He knew perfectly well that Balbir was a very shy young man. He had no *novia*, and certainly not a sophisticated one using expensive French scent.

"Where did you get that handkerchief?" he asked curtly.

"It is just something I happened to pick up, sir," stammered the unfortunate Balbir. Succumbing to the Commissioner's and Ambassador's relentless questioning, he told the story of the incident at the airport.

"Ah," said the Commissioner, "so you thought the lady was familiar, did you?"

"I swear I had never set eyes on her before, sir," said poor Balbir, "but at that time she did remind me of someone."

"Hmm. Not tall, dark complexion, long hair? Well, well." And with a pleased look on his face, the Commissioner got up and started to leave.

"Why should you be interested in a lace handkerchief?" asked the Ambassador, accompanying him to the door.

"Has it not occurred to you, Your Excellency, that the young lady of the airport sounds remarkably like your daughter, whose passport is missing?"

"This is ridiculous! My daughter is in bed – she has been most unwell this past month ever since my wife passed away. She has gone nowhere and she doesn't use scent. Her mother never allowed her to use any make-up or perfume."

"Quite right," the Commissioner soothed him. "Young girls don't need make-up. A pity so few realize it. I believe in India you have many ancient recipes for cosmetics. I read an article once..."

"Look here, Commissioner, never mind Indian recipes. My daughter's passport was lost while she was out riding. Very careless of her, certainly, but not a criminal act. It was reported. No one could have found it and made use of it because she went riding cross-country where one doesn't meet a soul. This smuggling business of yours can have no connection with my daughter or her passport."

"As you say, Excellency," smiled the Commissioner. "But we must collect all the facts for our investigations."

The Ambassador stood and stared at the door closing behind the Commissioner. Every time that wretched fellow came to see him he came up with some improbable nonsense and got him, a mild and reasonable man, all worked up. He turned to go to his desk and saw Balbir still standing in the middle of the room, very ill at ease.

"You may go, Balbir Singh," he said coldly. "Keep this matter confidential and in future don't make a habit of picking up young ladies' scented handkerchiefs."

Mona was preparing to leave her room at last. She knew she was behaving like a child but her deep sense of guilt would not be overcome. She had not been able to make herself leave this refuge and face the world. She had been so unhappy that day – it seemed like a year ago but was only three days before that fearful and terrible day – the day of the reception, the day of her mother's death.

For so long she had been unhappy and frustrated, hating her way of life. There was nothing for her at home. Her father's time was spent in office all day and at parties every evening; her mother's one goal seemed to be to remake Mona in her own image. She had no communication with either of them, nor had they any understanding of the person she really was beneath the docile daughter they saw at meals.

It was an intolerable situation and in a mood of rebellion she had gone off one afternoon, before the National Day reception, without telling her mother. She had driven with Gloria to a nearby village market. It was a weekly tradition: villagers of the surrounding area brought their produce for sale and barter. It was a very colourful market. Here one could find clay pots, hand-woven fabrics, goats, live chicken, quails and parakeets in small cages, baskets full of plump tomatoes and many varieties of chillies and avocados. In one section sat a row of old women, wrinkled, stern-looking hags, selling dried herbs and flowers for medicinal purposes and strange dried objects such as twigs and other things which were only known by their ancient names and were used for magic charms of various sorts. Some were love potions – these included concoctions to lower the resistance of the beloved. Others were intended to change a harsh personality to a more pleasant one.

With much whispering and giggling, Gloria and Mona had decided to consult a grim sorceress who sat immobile behind her wares. She was completely wrapped up in her *rebozo* and only her brown face, corrugated with deep wrinkles, was visible. They told her they wanted a mixture to calm an aggressive person and she listened to them in silence and then asked one or two questions. At last, she took a pinch of this and a pinch of that. She produced an ancient pestle and mortar from the folds of her clothes and ground the lot into a fine powder. Then she chanted an incantation over the charm in a low voice, in words they could not understand. She poured the powder into a piece of paper torn from some old newspaper, screwed it up and then placed it in a plastic bag. Mona told Gloria that the charm was for a joke and Gloria promised to keep her secret. But actually she planned to try it on Mama, to make her less angry.

After paying up, they spent the rest of the afternoon wandering around the market, eating tacos and making a great many unnecessary purchases. They drove home late in the afternoon with the car full of potted plants, ceramic mugs and various odds and ends.

They were well satisfied with their outing.

At home, Mona had arrived to find Savitri furious with her for having disappeared without a word. "And just when I need you to help me with a hundred and one things. There is so much to be done before the reception," she had said in a hoarse voice. She had been coming down with a cold and had planned to go to bed early. "I don't want to be sick on Republic Day," she said. "Mona, tell Gulati Singh to make me some banafsha and bring it to my room."

Mona had got the banafsha steaming hot from Gulati Singh and, on an impulse, had put the powdered charm into it. Then she had strained the lot and taken it to her mother.

"Delicious," Savitri had said, sipping the traditional Indian remedy for a cold. "This is made of dried violets you know, child. It is so much better than the antibiotics doctors keep prescribing nowadays." Savitri's cold was gone the next day and she had worked unceasingly for the next days to complete all the preparations before the fateful party.

But now Mona was tortured by the thought of what she had done. How could she have been so mad as to do a thing like that? What proof was there that the 'medicine' was safe? A packet of dried stuff – goodness knew what was in it. Gloria had said that these were all very old herbal medicines, very well-known in the country for centuries and today accepted even by some modern doctors.

"You'd be surprised," she had told Mona, "how many people like us, not peasants, use these things. They come to the old women in secret sometimes. I know someone who tried the love potion and said it worked!" Gloria had giggled and Mona had joined her. But thinking it over in the light of what had happened, Mona wondered if Gloria really knew what she was talking about. She had probably invented knowing people who used the charms.

How could I have done this? Mona asked herself for the

millionth time. I may as well have put pins in a voodoo doll and wished for my mother to die.

The whole thing had been a bit of a joke but the joke had turned on her in a macabre way. She was nothing less than a murderess, unfit to face decent people. But she realized she would have to get back to normal living. She could not spend the rest of her life locked up in her bedroom. Her father was so worried about her. The servants, good simple people, kept bringing her tempting food, and the warmth of their concern made her feel worse because, by her evil act, she had put herself beyond the pale of decency and affection. If only there was someone she could turn to, though not her father. He would recoil in horror at her unnatural behaviour.

There was Anil of course. She thought about him. Yes, perhaps he would be able to tell her what she must do. If necessary, she must be ready to speak to the police. She rose from her bed and went to splash her tear-stained face with cold water.

Ram Nath was also looking for Anil. There had been several phone calls for him during the day but Anil had left the house after breakfast and had only just returned. Just after he got back, the phone had rung but the caller had refused to give his name, as he had refused previously.

"Odd," thought Ram Nath, and went in search of Anil.

"Yes, who's speaking?" asked Anil when he got to the phone.

"It is I, sir, Gonzalez. You promised to introduce me to the Ambassador, if you recall, sir."

"I did no such thing. I want nothing to do with you."

"Sir, sir, I beg of you, be a little patient. It is a most pressing matter. Do reconsider. It concerns the daughter of His Excellency, apart from other matters of great interest. If you should wish to contact me I shall be available at the number I gave you."

"Now what?" thought Anil. What could this creature know concerning Mona? The matter of the boots was over and done with and the lost passport had long since been reported to the office. He went out into the garden to think things over and saw Mona sitting in one of the cane chairs. She was out of her room for the first time since that dreadful day and she looked very ill.

As Anil approached her she got up and walked towards him, saying in a voice that trembled, "Help me, please help me!" Before he could make any reply she was sobbing and clinging to him as if he were the one immovable object in a raging hurricane. He put one arm around her thin shoulders and held her close while he stroked her hair, speaking in a low voice as if to a sick animal or a child. He was dismayed by her hysterical state and feared for her, especially when she told him, between sobs, that she had caused her mother's death.

Gulati Singh, happening to look morosely out of the window at that moment, saw the scene. He turned around, a smile on his face for the first time in many days and started to tell Lupita and Ram Nath that it was remarkable that life and death were but a part of one cycle and that although God had seen fit to take Bibiji, he had arranged that Baby and Anil Sahib would be married. He tore a sheet of paper out of his account book, and taking his blunt pencil he started to compose a letter to his wife, who lived in a remote mountain village in the Indian Himalayas. He asked her to go to the temple and offer laddus in thanksgiving for Baby's future happiness.

TEN

Balbir Steps Out

Anil had had a very disturbed night and waking early, he determined to speak to the Ambassador at breakfast about the problems which had kept him awake and crept into his dreams when finally he had fallen asleep. He had to broach the subject of Mona's imminent nervous breakdown and also the matter of Gonzalez. If Gonzalez did indeed know something detrimental to Mona, her father was the obvious person to be told about it. As to what this could be, Anil could not hazard a guess. He had turned the matter over and over in his mind but could arrive at no conclusion.

He got ready and went to the dining room and was half-way through his plate of bacon and eggs when his host came into the room. Ram Nath appeared, quietly, with a slice of papaya. He stood behind the Ambassador's chair, ready to pour out his coffee.

Anil waited until the papaya was finished before starting to unburden himself. After all, the Ambassador ultimately had to be told about Mona, he reasoned to himself, and there was no point in waiting for the niceties of breakfast to be over with before bringing this up. He spoke at some length, disclosing Mona's fears as well as the strange story of his impromptu meeting with Gonzalez. When he had come to the end of his account, the Ambassador pushed back his chair and carefully folded his napkin before inserting it into its ring.

"Are you telling me that Mona is involved with someone called Gonzalez?" he asked, raising his eyebrows fastidiously and looking distastefully at Anil.

"No, no," Anil was appalled by the Ambassador's lack of understanding. Obviously he had not paid the least attention to what had been said. "This man says he must see *you* on a matter of importance, which also concerns Mona's passport."

"I refuse to meet such a shady character. In my position I have to be extremely careful. My dealings must always be above-board. In any case, I don't see people alone. For all serious discussions I have my Counsellor with me and I insist on an *aide mémoire* being prepared." He looked most displeased as he rose from the table.

"But considering Mona's state of mind," insisted Anil, also rising, "wouldn't it be worthwhile having a talk with this fellow? Just a brief meeting to reassure yourself that the matter is not of concern to the police, for instance."

"Under no circumstances. You may find out from this Gonzalez, if you wish, what this is all about. It can't possibly concern the police. If there is anything I should take steps about I shall ask Bhagwan to see this man. I shall certainly not have anything to do with such unorthodox dealings myself." The Ambassador started to leave the room. "I hope I can trust you, Anil, not to go around talking about Mona's imaginings. It could do us a good deal of harm." With that, he left abruptly.

Anil stood where he was, thinking what a very odd fish Mona's father was. Then he sat down and helped himself to another cup of coffee. This whole thing had to be thought out carefully. The old boy was going to be no help at all. If Gonzalez had refused to talk so far he was hardly likely to do so now. After all, why should he talk to Anil? He had been most insistent on seeing only the Ambassador. If Mona's name had not cropped up, Anil would gladly have sent Gonzalez to Timbuctoo. But Mona's recurring involvement with affairs which were also of concern to the police was very worrying. First the boots, then the passport, and now what? No, he had to pursue the matter to the end, whether or not her father approved.

Added to all this was Mona's genuine belief that she had poisoned her mother. That was all rot of course. He had tried to tell her that if a poison was going to work it would not wait for over 76 hours before doing away with its victim. Over and over he had assured her of her innocence and reminded her of the doctor's report, of his signing the official certificate listing cause of death as heart failure, in a patient whom he had been treating for heart trouble. Mona had not been wholly convinced but she had certainly calmed down and been able to listen and even to talk about the matter somewhat rationally.

Taking a drink of the cooling coffee, Anil realized with a jolt that if anyone had poisoned Savitri, her husband would be the most likely suspect. Come to think of it, the old boy was a lot more 'with it' since his wife had died. In some subtle way he was a different person. It was not only that he openly had a drink before dinner in the evening and no longer haunted his study. In many ways, he looked more alert. The other day Anil had seen him pouring over a catalogue of fine porcelain, a ball-point pen in his hand, with which he kept making frequent ticks.

Anil remembered suddenly how anxious Savitri had been about the apparent blood stain on the dagger. She had taken him into the study to point out what she thought was the tell-tale mark. Since Jorge's murder she had been increasingly nervous, fearing possible assassins or at the very least an armed robbery. She had even suggested asking the Police Commissioner to have the dagger checked at a laboratory.

Anil had seen a faint mark on one of the daggers but he had supposed it was tarnish; it was absurd to imagine otherwise. He had told Savitri that approaching the police with such a suggestion would naturally put all members of the household under suspicion. This had done the trick; she had been much struck by this idea – apparently the possibility of such a thing had not occurred to her – and she had agreed that it would be wiser not to mention the matter to the Commissioner. But now that he considered all that had transpired, *could* it have been blood, he wondered?

But what of motive: why should the Ambassador want to kill Jorge? The idea was absurd. The coffee was stone cold and Anil decided that it would be a good idea to go to the study and have another look at those daggers to shed some light on the current state of affairs.

In the study everything was freshly dusted, neat and tidy. On the desk some roses in a vase were delicately scenting the room. The daggers were polished and gleaming against the oyster-coloured wall paint. Anil could not remember which one it was that Savitri had pointed out to him. He examined each one carefully and thoroughly. There was no question of any stain, blood or otherwise, on any of them.

Balbir had taken to walking around the town in his free time. The serenity of his quiet life had been upset since the incident of the handkerchief and suddenly he felt confined to a limited world; he strained to broaden his horizons. He was no longer content to return from office to his one-room flat, to eat and go to bed early night after night. Nor were the Sundays spent with one colleague or another as satisfying as they used to be. He still visited his colleagues and was happy for the companionship, the talk and the games of flush or rummy and the food prepared by the kind wives who were always so good to him. But there must be more to life than a plate of gulab jamun, he said to himself. How he could find what he was seeking he could not say – he did not even know quite what he wanted – but many evenings, he would go for a walk on a street where he had not previously been.

One day, as he strolled in a fashionable shopping area he was struck by the window display of a famous silversmith; particularly by one exquisite silver pear placed on a black velvet cushion. He could not get over it. How different from the silver bazaar at home, consisting of a whole street of shops, each full of display shelves and cupboards bursting with finely wrought silver ornaments, filigree earrings, heavy bracelets, delicate anklets, necklaces, carved and engraved glasses, bowls and hundreds of other objects. Shop after shop of silver, more or less the same wares in each shop. And here was a window displaying just one beautiful pear made of silver!

One Saturday afternoon he had gone into a museum for the first time in his life and seen the remains of a civilization which ended hundreds of years ago – which made him think of his own country and her ancient history. He had even visited a bookshop and looked at the titles of books and later returned and bought one with colour illustrations on the art of the country he was living in. He had been appalled to discover how expensive it was but had recklessly bought it anyway. I'll do without the cinema for a bit, he had said to himself.

Tonight, he had decided to go for a walk in another direction along the same street, which had many restaurants. He had never been here before. Naturally he could not afford to enter these expensive restaurants but at this time of the night it was quiet, with hardly any traffic, making it a good place for a stroll.

Passing a restaurant with red curtains at the high round windows, he heard the plaintive strains of a guitar. It caught his attention and he stood still, listening to the sad melody. It was beautiful. He was tall enough to peer through the high window and he saw a young man in a red jacket playing a guitar. Near him sat a woman with a red shawl around her shoulders. Her face was turned the other way and Balbir Singh could not see whether she was young or old. Then she started to sing and he was unable to move. Softly at first and then louder, her voice rose in deep cadence. The haunting melody of the guitar was now a song of despair, rising up to the beams of the small room, spilling out into the street. Balbir was transported to another world, and though the words were unintelligible, he was stirred by the rich voice of the singer and the provocative rhythm of her song; they reminded him somehow of the poignant hill songs of India. He stood and listened, his eyes never leaving the musicians. Then the song ended and the applause which followed awoke him from his reverie.

He looked around the room and saw that there were people sitting at tables covered with red cloths and lit with candles. To his great surprise, one of them was a familiar-looking girl with dark hair lying loose on her shoulders, her eyes outlined with black, some glittery thing on her lids which shone in the candle light: the mysterious girl at the airport! He was sure it was the same one.

Her companion was a dark man with a small moustache. He was leaning towards her and playing with the strand of pearls around her neck. Yes, Balbir was sure it was the same girl. But how can she be here, he thought, it was only the other day that I saw her leaving the country. Why has she returned so soon? He wondered what she would say if he walked in now and returned her handkerchief!

But of course he no longer had it. The Police Commissioner who had made those awful jokes had put it into an envelope and taken it away with him. That interview in the Ambassador's office had been most embarrassing. What a fool he had looked and how his boss had glared at him. He went hot thinking of the whole episode. He had never done such a stupid thing before – and for it to come to light before the boss was terrible. He hoped there would be no adverse comment in his annual report.

He walked away from the window and continued on his way. What should he do about seeing that girl in town again – should he inform the Ambassador? He hesitated to do so because he held his boss in awe. Yet the Commissioner had been very interested and should be told that the girl had already returned to San Felice. Then it would be up to the police to trace her. And who was the man? He looked like an Indian, but so did many of the inhabitants of San Felice. Balbir had a sense of disquiet. Something should be done – but what?

Kwame stretched and yawned hugely. He felt he had been out of circulation for a long time. His work had absorbed him so totally that he had hardly had any sleep or food, lying on the office couch when his eyes refused to stay open and grabbing a sandwich and coffee or a glass of beer from time to time. The report that he had handed in this morning had been sensational enough to read like fiction and he had no idea if his boss would believe it. Apparently the smuggling ring he had been asked to investigate was more of an empire, with a small core, of which he had little knowledge so far, and far-flung tentacles. It was controlled from three, possibly four, centres and its raison d'être was diamonds. An army of young people were used as carriers for transporting gems from one country to another in amounts that ran into stupendous figures. It was not just a question of smuggling, this was Big Business.

The young carriers were mainly chosen for their credability as honeymooners – who would normally suspect two young people off on a wedding trip? But some were single men or women. Their function was to carry the diamonds to a certain city and they were handsomely paid to do so. They were contacted almost immediately and thereafter had a legitimate holiday before returning home. In past years this organization had flourished and even been responsible for endangering the economy of some states with the immense influx of contraband diamonds.

It was by coincidence that a carrier, a lovely young woman travelling alone, had been apprehended on suspicion of having heroin in her possession. The diamonds, skillfully concealed, had been found and an investigation had begun. Who would believe, Kwame thought, that a honeymoon couple or a girl who said she was going to find a guru in India would be large-scale smugglers? It was not as if these people were hippies. On the contrary they were affluent, the so-called beautiful people of the world, with time and money and first-class air tickets. The whole thing pointed to a very well-organized, intelligent operation.

Exhausted but exhilarated now that his report was handed in, Kwame felt alive and in need of company. He called up Mona and then Anil. Anil answered, asking him to come over to the house.

Kwame was led into the garden by Ram Nath. In the brilliant sun the grass was a deep green carpet and hummingbirds hovered over the fuchsia plants. Kwame had never been in the Embassy – knowing Mona's mother disliked him, he had always waited for her outside the gates. Now he looked around and took deep breaths of the clean, fresh air. Good to be out of the smoggy office, he thought.

Mona and Anil came out of the house and he saw that Mona was very thin and had dark circles around her eyes. He picked her up in a bear hug.

"Kid, you look like a skeleton. In my country they would send you to a fattening house," he said in a joking way, to prevent her from seeing how stunned he was by her appearance.

"What's a fattening house?" asked Anil, helping him dissemble. Kwame laughed.

"It's a wonderful tribal tradition," he said. "At about 15 or so, girls are fattened up by being kept in one room, given goodies to eat and massaged with special oils. When they are good and fat they're ready to get married!" He laughed again at Anil's amazement.

Mona smiled and, trying to rouse herself from her apathy, asked if he would like to have coffee or some beer.

"Thanks, no. That's what I've been living on for the last couple of weeks. I could eat a horse. What about coming out with me and having an enormous meal? We'll try and fatten you up in one session! I can't eat a huge lunch alone and unless I do so I am likely to collapse," grinned Kwame.

"Excellent idea," said Anil. "We could all do with a change." Mona was not interested in food or in going out but they both coaxed and teased her until she found herself smiling and went to fetch a sweater. With Mona away for the moment, Kwame asked Anil about his talk with Gonzalez and heard about that as well as the strange conversation at breakfast with Mona's father. Like Anil, he was taken aback but just then Mona returned to the garden. They piled into the yellow Beetle and drove off into the country, where a well-known inn they liked specialized in grilled food.

ELEVEN

Diamonds Forever

Bhagwan had been dealt a great blow. For the past weeks he had been feeling at ease – the death of the Count had freed him of worry about his wife and though he still had trouble sleeping and occasional headaches, the tension of earlier days had been relieved. He had received a foolishly dramatic anonymous note which he had ignored. But today the blackmailer had telephoned. He had demanded to know why Bhagwan had left town without getting in touch with him. Then, speaking in a more friendly way, he said, "Stop shilly-shallying or Sheela will be exposed – a meeting can be arranged, a congenial lunch or a drink at the Safari Club – these things should be done in a civilized manner, shouldn't they? What about setting a time?" When Bhagwan remained silent the hated voice continued, with an undertone of menace, "The sooner the better." Then the call was disconnected.

"How can this be?" Bhagwan raged inwardly. Jorge had been Sheela's lover, such playboys were known to be rakes. There had been no question of any other lover.

"I suppose I had better see this damned man and find out what this is all about. At least I'll be out of the dark then," he resolved, deciding to take the plunge. In any case, he did not yet even know where he came into the picture as far as the blackmailer's reckoning was concerned; what was going to be demanded of him. With great reluctance, but with a sense of inevitability, he picked up the phone again and dialled the number. With every fibre of his being in revolt, he managed to say, "You win. I'll meet you at the Safari this evening."

He rang for Nair and started to dictate. Work was piling up while his brain was in torment, and he could not concentrate on his office routine. Official work had always absorbed his time and his interest. Sheela used to tell her friends, "Bhagwan's first wife is the office, I'm only a poor second." And they used to laugh because Sheela was young and pretty and nobody could seriously believe that a husband would prefer the office to her company. The staff must never know how sick he felt. Others must not be aware that his mind refused to function. There would be a lot of unnecessary talk and conjecture as to why he was in this state – and at all costs Sheela's name must never be associated with any careless gossip. He tried to empty his mind of personal worries and was soon in full stride, dictating with his usual fluency.

In the meanwhile, at the Safari Bar, the tropical atmosphere was as overwhelming as ever. A few tables were occupied and three businessmen were sitting at the long bar, toasting the successful termination of an undertaking. Their loud laughter and cheerful calls for refills kept the barman busy.

Near an artificial pool with floating lilies and a stuffed alligator, sat a swarthy man. He smoked a Kent and stroked his moustache with the tip of a finger. From time to time he looked at the girl sitting at a table not far from him. She wore a wrap-around skirt made of local handicraft material with glittery threads in it and her shining dark hair was done up in a chignon. She sipped a dry martini and seemed unaware of the admiring looks cast her way. The swarthy man had explained to the maître d'hôtel that the young lady was with him – the Safari Bar did not encourage girls to sit alone at tables, it was not that kind of place – and the maître d'hôtel had understood that it would be very dull for the young lady to have to sit through a boring business talk. He had escorted her to a small banquette covered with a zebra skin and brought her a dish of olives to nibble on, with her drink.

"How adorable she is," thought the swarthy man as he smoked his cigarette and anticipated the date which awaited him. He wished Bhagwan would hurry up, but he gave no sign of his impatience.

He had called Sheela a couple of days ago but instead of her usual joyful agreement to a rendezvous, she had sounded flustered and launched into a long, implausible yarn about some women's club appointment which she had to keep that afternoon. She was not the kind who went to women's clubs and he had not been deceived for a moment. It was then that he had determined to put the screws on Bhagwan. He had called Bhagwan a few times last week but only once had anyone answered the phone. A vaguely familiar voice on the other end of the line had made him cautious and he had not spoken a word.

He had just finished his cigarette when Bhagwan came lumbering into the room, blinking a little as his eyes adjusted to the dim light of the bar. He looked around and a waiter came and took him to the table, as had been prearranged. He sat down and said abruptly, "What do you want from me?"

"Let's order first, my friend, you must be exhausted coming directly from office. What's your poison?"

"I allowed you to enter my house once against my better judgment," Bhagwan snapped, "but I won't drink with you here, you swine!" Then, at the look of ironic amusement on the other's face, he said sulkily, "Oh, all right, I'll have a soda water." A waiter was called and the order given.

"Let's get down to business. My proposition is very simple. All I want is to borrow your wife's passport for a few days – no more than a week at most."

Bhagwan looked at him with a poker face. "And you expect to use my wife's passport and her name for some criminal purpose. What do you take me for?"

"Nothing criminal, my dear chap. Just a short trip to New York for my secretary who has planned to holiday and wants to bring back some dutiable goodies – you know what women are like. I'd like to help her."

"I'm sure you would. And you think I am a fool enough to believe that you have been plaguing me for over a month to help your secretary evade customs!"

"It doesn't really interest me what you believe." The drinks had arrived and the man took a swallow of his whiskey and water while Bhagwan stared at the glass of iced soda in front of him. "However, it would be more comfortable for you if you did believe me." He grabbed a handful of nuts and started to crunch them. "Unless I have the passport by the end of the week I shall be forced to let your Ambassador know of the scandalous conduct of a member of his Embassy. I have some rather good photographs too of your lovely little Sheela. I am sure there must be rules of behaviour for diplomats and their wives. It will be the end of your career. I know men like you – even if the government looks the other way you'll be finished because you can't stand the idea of everyone knowing that Sheela is a…"

"Be quiet damn you, and don't take my wife's name!" Bhagwan was in a murderous rage. "My wife may have been led astray, but the man who did it is dead. I don't need to put up with your vulgarity and your damned impertinence!"

"Dead?" The hand that was reaching for more peanuts was arrested in motion.

"Yes. Count de la Bolla."

"The *Count?* Oh, you miserable fool!" The man burst into loud, uncontrollable laughter. People turned to stare at their table and looked away again. "What gave you that idea?" he asked, when he had managed to restrain his mirth.

Bhagwan was rigid with disgust. And he was furious. "You are a contemptible cad and I want nothing more to do with you. Since you have been ogling that tramp at the next table constantly, why don't you ask her to join you? I'm leaving." He pushed back his chair and strode to the door.

"That's just what I had in mind," the swarthy man called after him, beginning to roar with laughter once more.

Mona was better. She had started attending classes once more and even made an attempt to eat a little at meals. The servants fussed over her and the women of the Embassy came over to the house to keep her company. She looked like a waif, and still seemed to walk about in a trance most of the time.

Anil felt that he must do something to prove that she was not guilty of her mother's death. He had no idea how to go about getting this proof but the alternative was to let Mona limp through life, an emotional cripple.

However, there was nobody who could advise him. He had thought of Bhagwan, but the poor man looked like a zombie and remembering that distasteful piece of paper he had come across, Anil could guess why. The Ambassador of course was out of the picture.

Kwame. He made up his mind, deciding to rope in just about the only person he could trust to get involved.

They met in town and went to eat in a shabby café that Kwame recommended, which specialized in a hearty chicken soup. At practically no cost you could get a large dish of boiling chicken broth to which were added pieces of chicken, rice, bits of tortillas, slices of avocado, minced onions, green chillies and various other tasty ingredients. It was satisfying and Kwame said he could manage several helpings if he was ravenous.

"Suggest some way out of this dead end," Anil said,

spooning soup into his mouth. "Mona is in danger of becoming a permanent wreck."

"What about getting that junk from the old witch and having it analysed by a chemist? That should prove that it's not poisonous at any rate."

"Yes, we could do that. Let's take Mona to the market now so we get the right stuff." They finished their meal and were about to leave when a tentative touch on his arm made Anil turn. Gonzalez stood there, obsequious as ever.

"Have you been following me around?" demanded Anil, angrily.

"What makes you think that, sir? I often come here for a dish of *caldo de pollo*. Seeing you, I did wonder if you had mentioned my little request to the Ambassador?"

"Look, drop the whole thing, will you? He won't see you, so just forget it."

"Why don't we do a little deal with Gonzalez ourselves?" Kwame said suddenly. He had a hunch that there might be something interesting in the man's insistence. "Let's sit down again and talk this over."

They returned to their table. The lunch hour was over and the room was empty. "Since the Ambassador doesn't care to see you I think you should let us in on your secret," Kwame told Gonzalez firmly, leaving no room for argument in his manner.

The man appeared to consider the matter. It did not seem probable that he would be able to meet the Ambassador. And these two might be able to deliver the goods.

"I have information," he said at last, "which could be of great use to your government." He looked at Anil. "But I cannot divulge the nature of the business until I have a guarantee that I shall be paid my price for doing so." He paused. "I also know where the passport of His Excellency's daughter is."

"Where is it?"

"That I cannot at present tell you, sir."

"Well, what is your price for all this information?" asked Anil, and Gonzalez named a staggering sum in American dollars.

"For that amount I could buy the Taj Mahal and live in it," Anil protested.

"That was my intention also, sir," answered Gonzalez, "but not the Taj Mahal, of course. I have heard about it and I doubt if it could be turned into a family residence."

"Oh, for God's sake." Anil swore, in disgust.

Meanwhile Kwame was lost in thought. "How can we arrange for you to be paid by any government unless we know what you have to offer?" he asked Gonzalez at last.

"That is very true," Gonzalez pondered the matter at length. At last he made up his mind. "I will tell you. I trust you though my life is in danger if you make known anything I am going to say." And he proceeded to tell them some extraordinary facts very relevant to the report Kwame had submitted recently to his boss.

"How can you possibly know this?" Kwame asked, staring at Gonzalez in utter astonishment. It was incredible but, if what this man had been saying was indeed true, it was dynamite.

"How do we know you are connected with the traffic of illegal diamonds," Anil wanted to know, "and if you are, why are you betraying your companions?"

In response, Gonzalez put his hand in his pocket and took out a small leather pouch that closed with drawstrings. He opened it and tipped the contents onto the table. The scarred table top glittered with the gems scattered all over it.

"Blue diamonds," Gonzalez whispered in a soft voice, as the two young men stared at the jewels. They had never seen anything like it. "Take one, sir," he said. "I would like you to have one. My pleasure. Take it as a pledge of my sincerity. As to your other question, I have been duped by my one-time comrade and I will not stand for it. Those who play me false must pay for it."

Anil and Kwame, looking at his grim expression, were struck by the change in the man. He was no longer the rather greasy Gonzalez they had become used to. Here was a ruthless personality. They believed him.

"Put away your diamonds. We'll be in touch with you shortly," Anil told him, and he left the restaurant with Kwame. He needed to get away quickly. Above all, he needed time to think and to consult someone. Kwame could go to his boss but there was no one in whom he, Anil, could confide. God, what a mess, he thought, as he wended his way home.

TWELVE

No Rest for Police Commissioners

The Commissioner was very tired. None of the leads he had followed so far had taken him anywhere in his murder investigation. With the smuggling business as well, they seemed to have arrived at an impasse. Of course that was a highly confidential matter and the press had no idea that investigations were being made into an illegal worldwide empire. The only journalist in the picture was that African chap with the U.N. but he was in a different category and sworn to secrecy. It would be detrimental to the inquiry if anything leaked out. The solution of the murder, however, was another matter. The international media was practically at his doorstep, full of pressing conjecture and curiosity. Interest in the Count's death had not flagged for a single day.

The Commissioner's reputation was at stake, but apart from official considerations, he was also personally involved. After all, Jorge had been a close friend. A fun-loving man, generous to a fault, certainly with a few of the foibles and vices which were part of his inheritance, along with his vast wealth and considerable property. He had to see this murder avenged and he would do it. But at the moment, he was exhausted.

He got into a pair of trunks and went into the garden. The pool looked inviting and he dived in neatly at the deep end.

Nothing like exercise to keep a man trim and in good humour, he thought when he had completed several lengths. He pulled himself out of the water and dried himself with a jumbo-sized towel. The pool was heated but the evening breeze could be treacherous. He dressed quickly in slacks and a light sweater. He had had a large midday meal so he was not hungry, but he craved a tequila. He rang for his man servant who entered the room and put a tray before him containing a carafe of the colourless liquid, a small glass, a wedge of lemon and some salt. He took a sip of the drink, licked some salt off the back of his hand and sucked the lemon. This is the only way to drink tequila, he thought. Cocktails are for *gringos*. The strain and fatigue of the day drained away and he began to relax.

Just then, the doorbell rang. He was annoyed to see his butler come in and announce that Pepe was here to see him. Pepe entered at once. The young man was the son of dear friends and entitled to walk into the house at any hour but the Commissioner was not pleased today.

Not tonight, he thought with a sigh. He had looked forward to putting on a record of a Mozart quartet and having a very light, quiet supper on his own. Nevertheless, he rose with habitual grace and welcomed Pepe.

Pepe's manner was very subdued. Even his clothes lacked their normal panache. Without the least drama, he shook hands and got to the point.

"Gloria has just told me something quite terrible," he said, "and I felt I had to let you know about it immediately." He gave the Commissioner the gist of what Gloria had said about her visit to the village market with Mona for the purchase of the magic potion. "She said that Mona had asked her to keep it a secret. It was a joke. But now Gloria has been wondering if the thing was meant for Mona's mother. It was a medicine to make angry people nicer, you know, and Mona's mother was always getting angry with her, poor thing. Suppose she gave it to her mother and her mother died of it? This is what is upsetting poor Gloria. She promised Mona she wouldn't tell anyone but she is so scared that she came to my place tonight to get it off her mind. She is there still."

The Commissioner's fatigue vanished. He sat up straight in his chair as Pepe told his story. He had thought it odd that the Ambassadress had fallen dead like that. She had been fit as a fiddle at the reception, and now here was potential proof that his suspicions were justified. He had remarked on her energy, and had questioned the doctor very closely after the event, without telling the bereaved husband. But the doctor had assured him that in the case of some heart patients such a sudden death was not uncommon. Then again, doctors hated to commit themselves. Their talk was camouflaged with medical jargon difficult for a layman to understand. The information brought by Pepe put an entirely different aspect on the cause of death and would have to be looked into. To imagine that demure little thing capable of such a deed! It made the head reel. For all he knew the 'medicine' was not at all what Gloria thought it was but something that had been purchased to do away with a hated person. Such occurrences were only too common as he, a policeman, well knew. But usually such cases were crimes of passion. For a daughter to get rid of her mother – and in the diplomatic service at that! Was there no end to his problems? One murder at a time was more than enough for anyone.

He made Pepe repeat the story to be certain he had the facts correct. Then he asked him to go and fetch Gloria and again he went over every detail, making a few notes. Whether he liked it or not, he would have to take official cognisance, and what a stink there would be. He thought of the riding boots – they had been found with fingerprints smudged all over them and those foolish police at Jorge's house had handled them so much that it was impossible to tell to whom the prints belonged. Then there was the mystery of the lost passport. Could it possibly be that, in spite of all she had said, Mona was indeed implicated in Jorge's murder? It seemed absurd to think so, but such things did happen. Perhaps she had been madly in love with Jorge – a first love affair could release latent passions – and suppose something went wrong, would she have turned to murder? Surely not in this case. Such a dear little thing she seemed. But dear little things had been known to murder. On the day of the reception she had presented a charming picture in her bright sari. Sentimentally, he had thought of her as a delightful tropical bird. Now he would have to question her and the father would not like that. Oh no, His Excellency would not like it at all! He knew that the Ambassador disliked him, though he hid his feelings well beneath his polished manners.

The Ambassador was a dark horse and rather a chirpy dark horse since he had become a widower. Everyone had noticed this. What if, alternately, he had had a hand in his wife's death? Did Savitri have property or substantial money that *he* would now inherit? Or, who knows, he may have had a mistress. More than likely and after all quite natural, thought the Commissioner, casting his mind back on various amorous affairs which had made his life agreeable. Perhaps Savitri had found out and forced the poor fellow to take drastic steps. Whom could he tackle to find out something about His Excellency's private affairs? The obvious person would have been Jorge – he had always had a fund of knowledge about all his friends.

Suddenly he recalled Anil, the young man at the Embassy who had been such a help to him. He had thoroughly enjoyed his story about murder, *Death by Defection*, all about politicians defecting to opposing parties and being poisoned by sweets offered after they were sworn in as cabinet ministers. Quite absurd, even for India, and of course incorrect police procedure, but a good yarn nevertheless.

"Is that young man still at the Indian Embassy?" he asked the two young people, Pepe and Gloria, who had sat in uneasy silence while he was lost in thought. "I think I will see him tomorrow."

He did not want to get involved in talk of diplomatic immunity and all the other things he knew the Ambassador would bring up. Better check all the facts with the young man first. He was probably affianced to the young girl in any case, and perhaps Gloria had got things wrong.

The Ambassador was in his office opening the mail contained in the bag. One letter held his attention and he read it over twice before sending for his Counsellor. In a little while Bhagwan came in, his suit crumpled and dark patches under his eyes. It occurred to the Ambassador that Bhagwan was not looking his calm and stolid self these days.

"Anything wrong?" he asked. "You're looking off-colour, Bhagwan."

"No sir. I'm fine. Got to bed rather late last night," lied Bhagwan.

"Ah, so that's it," said the Ambassador, never an observant man. "You young people have all the fun parties while we old fogies have to do the dull official round. I envy you!" He handed Bhagwan the letter. "Have a look at that. Curious, isn't it, in view of what the Commissioner was saying the other day."

The letter pertained to suspicion of jewel smuggling, particularly of diamonds, which had come to the surface as a result of Interpol inquiries within the last weeks. All missions had been alerted and some specific instructions had been sent to the Embassy at San Felice. "Take care of this, will you?" the Ambassador said to Bhagwan, turning to his other mail.

Bhagwan returned to his office and sent for Balbir. He remembered that he had not checked on further developments over the missing passport. In case someone was using Mona's passport, all relevant authorities had been informed of its number and any person presenting it would be detained instantly and the passport confiscated.

The consular officer came in, looking smart and alert. Today his turban was plum-coloured. Bhagwan gave him a jaundiced look. A splendid specimen, certainly, but why did he have to look so healthy? He made his queries in a harsh voice. Balbir gave him the latest update. No word had been received so far and the passport was genuinely lost.

It occurred to him, mid-report, that this was a good time to inform the Counsellor about the girl at the airport and the Commissioner's interest in her. He went on to mention that he was certain that he had seen her in a restaurant a couple of nights ago. Naturally, he did not mention the handkerchief. Even after all this time he blushed to think of it, but he had been fascinated by that handkerchief as much as by the heady perfume with which it had been drenched. He had never before seen such an object. The handkerchief used by his sisters and his mother were at least six inches square and were hand-embroidered with pink and blue flowers or designs of lover's knots or sometimes even miniature gardens. He had never dreamed that such a frivolous thing existed as that girl's bit of muslin and lace. How could a girl blow her nose on a piece of lace?

Bhagwan listened impatiently to the involved story of some girl in a restaurant but it did not seem to make much sense. So what? he thought. If that idiotic policeman wants to go about finding a female he has the entire police force to help him. I have problems enough of my own. He dismissed Balbir with little ceremony and turned his attention to his official mail.

THIRTEEN

H.E. Not Amused

"How could you, Gloria!" Francisca, normally a very placid woman, was furious. She had just heard of Pepe's and Gloria's visit to the Commissioner and had flown into a temper. Gloria was alarmed. This was so unlike Francisca that her big eyes filled with tears. But she was quite resolute. After all, why should she not have gone to the police?

"I had to go – I was so unhappy over the whole thing and when Pepe suggested that we speak to the Commissioner, it seemed the only thing to do. Who else can handle it?"

"And so, without a word to Mona who is supposed to be your friend, you dashed off to accuse her of killing her mother! Bravo! And where does Pepe come into it? We all know he has been longing for the police to take notice of him – he's been making a real exhibition of himself for weeks and now you have given him a chance to be taken seriously."

Gloria remained silent.

"I don't think I can stand being in the same room with you for another minute. I'm going to go to Mona right now and warn her."

Mona was struggling with the household accounts and Gulati Singh was standing by with his usual inane look. This was a chore her father would never dream of doing so she had to take over the responsibility of their domestic finances. The trouble was that she could never get a correct total for the figures in the account book. Each time the answer was different and Gulati Singh, with his indulgent talk, made her feel about five years old. She was relieved to see Francisca ushered into the room by Ram Nath and told Gulati, "I'll do this hisab later."

"What about what's owing to me, Baby?" he asked and she took some notes from her bag and handed them to him.

"What about lunch, Baby?" he persisted. "Shall I make English or desi?

"Make what you like, make anything."

Gulati looked at the notes in his hand and counted them carefully. Then he began to smile happily. At last, the money he had spent on Conchita's earrings had been made good. There were very nice nylon shirts in the market. He had noticed one with fruit all over it – a design of bananas, cherries and pineapples, that would be a good buy, he decided.

The girls went up to Mona's room where they would not be disturbed and Francisca burst out with an account of the dreadful conduct of Gloria and Pepe.

"I don't know what came over Gloria and I do apologise for her but I want you to be prepared for the police, Mona. They are bound to come around and ask questions and it's going to be so awful for you."

She had expected Mona to be alarmed, frightened, angry, at any rate to show *some* emotion. But Mona remained unnaturally calm. She listened to Francisca in silence, feeling grateful for this end to her dilemma. Anil had not been helpful at all. Although she kept telling him that her guilt was a matter of thought and not necessarily deed, he refused to listen. The charm may not have been poison but it could have harmed Mama anyway. But Anil was so stubborn that he went on insisting that the charm had nothing to do with the tragedy. In the end, he refused to discuss the matter with her any further.

"Life is not what it appears on the surface," Mona said thoughtfully. "I loved my mother, I really did, yet I tried, even if by accident, to harm her and perhaps I really have killed her. And look at Pepe telling the world that he was involved in some way in Jorge's murder."

"Pepe is an ass," Francisca said firmly. "I have no idea if Jorge was a homosexual. I doubt it, though. Anyway I am not interested. I couldn't care less. There's too much talk of all these private things in the open nowadays and I don't like it. But Pepe I've known since he was a boy and he loves to dramatize everything, including himself. I'm sure he invented the whole story to be the hero of the day and get into the limelight. I could shake him."

"But why?"

"Who knows? Perhaps he wished it had happened and now has convinced himself that it did. I do wish he'd grow up. I don't mind his trying to look like Little Lord Fauntleroy but this mud-slinging is too much. I'm not going to stand for any more. Do you know what I've just thought of? I'm going to tell his grandmother all about his stupid behaviour. She lives in the country and probably hasn't heard all the town gossip. She'll put an end to his making a laughing stock of himself." Francisca was cheered by the bright idea and left, glad that Mona had taken the shattering news so well.

Bhagwan was on edge. He was sleeping badly again and taking the sleeping pills the doctor had prescribed, but still he grew more irritable every day. And the days were chasing one another, a new one starting before it seemed possible that the last had ended. Or so it seemed to him. As if a deadline had to be kept by the end of the week. That was when the Ambassador would receive a letter, probably sent anonymously, with pictures of Sheela and X. Who was X? That blackguard had laughed like a hyena when he had mentioned the Count, as if he knew for sure that the Count had not been Sheela's lover. Then who on earth could it be? Mentally he reviewed the list of all their friends and acquaintances and tried to imagine Sheela with a treacherous but faceless person. He could not fit any face into the picture. It was a painful exercise and quite fruitless. Of one thing he was sure – that letter must be intercepted at all costs. But Bhagwan did not for a moment consider handing over Sheela's passport. He had done many things in his life that he regretted deeply, but he could not be intimidated in this way. He would never submit to blackmail. Sheela must be protected. And what about him? His entire career was at stake.

He had given instructions that all local mail coming to the Chancery should be brought to him first before distribution. To the surprised Nair he had given some vague explanation about terrorists and bombs concealed in letters. Nair had suggested that such a sensational idea was far-fetched but Bhagwan had been adamant. He realized that he should also check on the private mail going to the Ambassador's residence. He could take neither Anil nor Mona into confidence nor could he tell them the yarn about terrorists. It would be better to speak to the servants who collected the mail, in any case. He rang up the residence and Gulati answered with a thunderous, "Hello?" nearly splitting Bhagwan's eardrum.

"I want to speak to Ram Nath," Bhagwan said, holding the receiver a foot away from his aching ear. Gulati was too stupid to be entrusted with the task of watching for the postman.

"He is not here, Sahib," yelled Gulati. "He has gone shopping to look for a good papaya. I told Baby we need papaya every day for Sahib's breakfast but she is such a child she does not remember. This morning I had to send melon to Sahib and he only ate half of it. I told Ram Nath that I would go myself to the market to find a really ripe papaya. Sahib only likes the red ones, he doesn't care for the yellow variety. But Ram Nath insisted on going. He had to get razor-blades in any case. You know, Bibiji used to make us shave every single day and she gave us blades, but now we don't like to mention the matter to Sahib and Baby forgets what we tell her. Even the matter of the papaya, I told her only yesterday… hello?"

I'll have to see Ram Nath myself, thought Bhagwan and slammed down the receiver in disgust.

"That's funny," Gulati said aloud. "Who could have disconnected the phone?"

In the downtown office of the U.N., Kwame had just finished a long talk with his superior officer and had been briefed on what he had to do. For the last two days discussions had been going on at a high level about the diamond probe and, at one point, Kwame had feared that the sheer improbability of his report and the information given by Gonzalez would make his superiors dismiss the whole thing out of hand. But eventually a consensus had been reached and Kwame had been told to go ahead and negotiate with Gonzalez. He was elated and went off to inform Anil before their appointment with Gonzalez. The rendezvous was at the soup place, a spot not likely to be catering to customers at this hour, well before lunchtime.

Gonzalez was waiting for them. He had shed his previous oily manner and was easier to cope with. Clearly and concisely, he gave them information: a name, a passport number, a date, the amount of contraband being carried and its value. The person would be passing through Calcutta in transit to Bangkok and a very careful search would reveal much of interest to the authorities. If the search proved worthwhile, Gonzalez would expect his due and be prepared to give further information as and when the occasion arose.

Calcutta! That meant that the Ambassador must be informed immediately so that local authorities could work with Interpol. Anil wondered, with a sinking feeling, how he could get through to the Ambassador to make him see the urgency of the situation. He decided the best thing would be to seek an interview with him at the Chancery.

Although there was not much work for the Ambassador during office hours, he kept himself busy. These days he was occupied with the perusal of catalogues and had been looking through one of Rosenthal china when Anil's request for an interview was brought to him. He was not pleased, but it was getting on for lunchtime and he thought he may as well see what the young man wanted.

Anil came in and the Ambassador sat in bewildered silence while he was forced to listen to a harangue about smugglers and police. He cut Anil short. This sort of thing was most annoying. He was not here to catch smugglers. His work lay in the political field and in the writing of reports with due thought given to style and the turn of a phrase. He had no desire to play cops and robbers or to get mixed up with the underworld. The idea was preposterous. He told Anil so in no uncertain terms.

"But, sir, the matter is of vital importance. Our police have to be informed so that the trap can be sprung. Surely you could send a telegram or something so that necessary steps may be taken?"

"Don't teach me my job, my boy," said the Ambassador, evenly. "I have been in this profession longer than you have been in the world."

"I don't claim your experience, sir," Anil was taken aback by the Ambassador's attitude. "But I do feel that we must take note of Gonzalez's statement and..."

"What?" The Ambassador sat up. "That Gonzalez again?

Exposure to low elements of society is making you rash, my boy. The last time you mentioned that man's name to me was in connection with Mona. If I recall correctly, you implied that Mona was mixed up with the chap and I'll tell you straight, Anil, I resent that kind of talk."

"Mona is not known to Gonzalez. Gonzalez has merely said that he knows where Mona's passport is and I should think you would want to have that information."

"Of course I want to have it. But if he knows where it is he should contact my consular clerk. Why bring me into it? If you persist in speaking of such unpleasant matters, I suggest you go over to Bhagwan's office and tell him. But I advise you to sleep on it. By tomorrow you may well see the futility of the whole thing. And be careful whom you meet socially. That a man is judged by the company he keeps is a maxim that holds true." The Ambassador dismissed Anil with a wintry smile and went back to his Rosenthal catalogue with obvious relief.

Anil left the room thoroughly baffled at H.E.'s obstinacy and his lack of comprehension. He was about to go to the Counsellor's room when the receptionist sent word that she was holding a call for him. The Commissioner was most anxious to see him as soon as possible on a matter of great urgency. What reply should she give?

Anil decided to postpone his meeting with Bhagwan and go to the Commissioner immediately.

FOURTEEN

Encounter with a Movie Buff

The Commissioner's office was most impressive. Anil had been asked to wait a few minutes in a huge ante-room and had then been escorted into a room that was even vaster. The police headquarters were in a former palace and the chief's room, thought Anil looking around him with awe, must have been the banquet hall. It had several large crystal chandeliers and many full size portraits of dull-looking personages from the last few centuries, going back to the conquistadores who founded San Felice. He had to cross acres of carpet to shake the Commissioner's hand. The Commissioner was most cordial.

"Ah, my friend from the East," he said. "I thank you for making yourself available so soon. Do sit down." Anil did so and waited. "The last time we had a chance to talk I remember we had a nice conversation about your beautiful country and the zenanas. So many curious customs! Fascinating for us. In that film of the Jules Verne book – I forget the name at the moment, there was a thrilling scene of a young and beautiful girl about to be burnt on her husband's funeral pyre, but in the nick of time she was rescued by David Niven. It was all very well done. Do you know the film? But perhaps you are too young to have seen it."

Anil admitted to having seen *Around the World in 80 Days*. He hardly remembered much of it though, for it had been during his school days in Nainital and the monsoon rain pounding on the tin roof of the cinema hall had made the soundtrack inaudible. It had been like going to a silent movie, except for the drumming of the rain overhead, and he only remembered laughing and talking with his friends while a series of pictures unfolded on the ancient screen. He wondered why the Commissioner had summoned him to discuss old movies and exactly where this talk was leading.

"Well, to business," said the Commissioner, as if reading his mind, and asked Anil if he knew anything at all about Mona's visit to the market. Anil said he knew everything and told him. He also informed him, since it was bound to come out, about Mona's fears and her near-breakdown as a result of her feelings of guilt. The Commissioner nodded.

"Very understandable." He looked serious. "So there was a strained relationship between mother and daughter?"

"Nothing of the sort," answered Anil indignantly. "Why, Aunty was the soul of kindness and Mona was devoted to her mother. The whole thing was a bit of a joke."

"Aunty?" the Commissioner asked in an interested voice. "So the families are related? I was under the impression that perhaps you were *novios*, you and the young lady, an alliance arranged in the cradle according to the custom of your Hindu religion…"

"Certainly not!" Anil was really annoyed at the old man. "I mean, we are not engaged and it is not our custom to engage babies while they're in their cradles."

"But I had the understanding that all marriages in India were arranged like this, not in the cradle perhaps, but by families?"

"Not all," said Anil nastily. "Sometimes we marry through advertisement."

A new vista seemed to open for the Commissioner, but before

he could embark on the story of a Hollywood extravaganza revolving around a matrimonial bureau in the exotic but peculiar East, Anil spoke again.

"What was your intention, sir, in view of this charm having been taken by the Ambassadress?"

"We must have an order of exhumation passed immediately and an autopsy must be performed as soon as possible," answered the Commissioner, very official all at once.

"That's impossible! Surely you know that the body was cremated?" Anil could not help adding, perversely, "According to the custom of our country."

"What?" the Commissioner was completely deflated. Despite the film he had seen about that terrifying funeral pyre he had never given a thought to such an alien manner of disposal of the dead. It was barbaric! Surely all civilized people followed the rite of burial? He had been banking on an autopsy to prove the cause of death conclusively and at one stroke his plans had collapsed.

Anil saw his face fall and felt sorry for him, though not very sorry. Having to cope with both murder and the unknown quantity that was the mystic East must be very frustrating for foreigners. He tried to save the situation a little, however, in view of the investigation at hand.

"A friend of mine had suggested that we get hold of the medicine that Mona brought home from the market and have it analysed. Then, at any rate, we would know for sure if there was any poisonous substance in the ingredients. If not, surely there can be no question of an unnatural death."

"Yes, a good idea. I was thinking along these lines myself." The Commissioner looked brighter as he pressed the intercom button and sent for his assistant. He gave orders that a sample of every magic potion being sold in the market must be purchased and each one analysed separately and with care in the government laboratory. He wanted the reports on his table within twenty-four hours. "And I will stand no delay!" he shouted, thumping the desk.

"But, sir," quailed his assistant, "I am afraid you have overlooked the fact that the village markets meet only once a week, and this particular one will not happen until Thursday. We have to wait for four more days."

"Very well, very well, then wait. But once you have the samples, I want no excuse and no delay." He turned a smiling face to Anil. "We shall soon have the facts with the help of science. No need to alarm the young lady. Unless there is definite evidence of poison in the report, I feel it is better to keep her out of things, and His Excellency too, of course. Why worry them unnecessarily?" he asked magnanimously.

Anil was very thankful to get away from this interview. At one point he had feared that the Commissioner's sense of obligation to his job would compel him to send for Mona to be questioned – and that silly girl would probably break down and confess to murder.

In the office of a large travel agency, a number of men and women were waiting while their tickets for travel abroad were prepared by girls behind the counter. Telephones kept ringing and people were coming in and going out into the street. Large colourful posters showing the playgrounds of the world hung on the walls and a big table was covered with travel magazines and airline timetables. One of the women behind the counter called out a name and a girl with neatly coiled hair put down the magazine she was glancing at and went up to get her ticket. "Everything is in order," smiled the travel agent as she handed a slim envelope to the customer. "Happy landing, and have a good time in Bangkok."

The girl put the ticket away in her shoulder bag and went out of the office. Her Mustang was parked around the corner and she walked to it and drove to the building which housed the offices of New World Export Import Inc. She was shown into the room of the managing director. He looked up with a slight frown from behind a large executive desk and said, "You shouldn't have come here. Business matters only in the other place. You know the rules." Then he smiled and went up to give her an embrace. "All set?"

She nodded.

"You'll have to be careful this time. There has been a slight delay in getting the diplomatic passport but we'll have it in time for the next trip. Where is the other passport? The one you used last time?"

"Romano said to give it to him."

"Who the devil is Romano?"

She described him. "Oh, that one," he said. "I know him better as Gonzalez. He's a nobody." Gonzalez was a pain in the neck but far too low in the set-up to be worth another thought. He had once tried to get too ambitious and been beaten down. Since then he had given no trouble. "OK, we'll get it from him. Unfortunately it can't be used again, it's too hot. As a lark I may even return it to the owner!" and he laughed heartily.

"You must destroy it," said the girl, in a serious tone. "I was going to do it myself when I got home but this Romano met me at the airport and said I was to give it to him." She looked disturbed.

"Don't worry your pretty head about it. I shall see to it personally. But it must be destroyed by now." He was in a very good mood. Everything was going according to plan, plus he had good reason to expect Sheela's passport in time for the next big trip. Bhagwan would never take the chance of having his wife exposed – he simply hadn't got the guts! What a joke that had been the other day at the Safari Club – he hadn't laughed so much in an age. The evening had ended well, he remembered, looking again at Dolly. Luck was still running his way – and why not? It was not as if he believed in the stars; he planned and organized carefully and intelligently. That was all that was required for success in life; his career was living proof of the fact. He looked at his watch. Getting on for two o' clock – time for lunch.

"Let's go out and have a bang-up lunch," he said, taking the girl's arm and moving towards the door. "Champagne, the works. We won't be seeing one another for a whole week."

Sheela and Mona were lunching together at the Narains' place. Mona had never cared for Sheela and the latter had rarely had time for the young girl. In any case she was not the type for girlish confidences and women's lunches. But since Savitri's death she had felt very sorry for Mona and had made it a point to spend time with her. Though Mona was not alone much because her friends were always coming over and the Embassy women were so kind. They would come to see her with a dish of some delicious food specially prepared for her or a sweater someone had knitted for her. Mona was grateful for their affection but she was so nervy these days that she could hardly be polite or make conversation. So she preferred being with Sheela, who was very casual, did not ask questions and never said in a hurt tone, "You don't take?" when Mona refused to eat something which was offered.

As for Sheela, in the past week she had done some serious thinking. The shock over the passport had made her realize with a jolt that she was mad to continue her butterfly existence. It was sheer luck that she had got by so far. Supposing someone had found out, or if Bhagwan had had the least suspicion? It was a sobering thought. She knew the affair was over when she got no further calls and could only be thankful that things had just fizzled out instead of ending with an explosion or scenes and recriminations, as read about in novels. That would have been too ghastly. She had been very fortunate and did not intend to do such an asinine thing again. Not in San Felice, she amended.

She had made club sandwiches and iced coffee and took them out into the small garden where Mona was bending over the only rose plant in the garden. They took their food under the shade of a tree and sat on the grass to have a picnic.

"You've pricked your finger, Mona, that rose bush has very sharp thorns. Here, take a paper napkin." She handed her one. "The other day, after ages, I was going through Bhagwan's clothes to see if that lazy Conchita had pressed his suits and I found a peculiar stain on one of his white dinner jackets. I couldn't get it clean and had to send it to the dry cleaner. When I asked how he got such a spot he said it may have been from rare meat at a dinner party. So you'd better not get any blood on your pretty sari. Dry cleaners here aren't all that good are they?"

"Goodness, however could Bhagwan stain his clothes with blood from the roast?"

"It wasn't much – they had that very rare meat at the buffet. You know how bloody the meat is here. I don't see how they can eat it. It used to make me sick when I first saw it served that way in Europe. All that raw-looking meat at dinner parties. Ugh!"

"I know," Mona laughed, "and lobsters with their whiskers on!"

Sheela was pleased to hear Mona laugh after so long. "You know, I can't imagine why Bhagwan took the meat at all. He can't bear it under-done. He's always saying 'Give me dal-roti any day!'"

They had another laugh over Bhagwan's oft-repeated saying.

"I expect a waiter just served it to him. You know how it is at a buffet. One gets such a lot of food put on one's plate."

They went on to more interesting topics of conversation. Mona wondered if Sheela could suggest some interesting books for her to read. Sheela subscribed to a book club and usually had the latest novels. They chatted pleasantly, finding comfort in the peaceful garden with their thoughts far from the recent traumatic past.

FIFTEEN

Solving Puzzles

Kwame came over to see Anil after dinner. It was the first time he had done such a thing and he hesitated to come to the Embassy uninvited but in the end he decided to risk it.

The Ambassador had been sitting with a pile of books in the drawing room, marking pages here and there with a ballpoint pen, and Mona and Anil had been in the middle of a game of Scrabble. When the Ambassador saw Kwame being brought in by Ram Nath he looked surprised and alarmed. He knew his wife had worried about Mona's friendship with the young African and, he thought, with reason. I hope there's no hanky-panky going on, he said to himself. Best thing I could do would be to pack Mona off to one of her brothers. He beat a quick retreat from the room and called after Mona to help him look for something he had misplaced in his bedroom. Mona left, calling to the others, "Don't talk about anything interesting while I'm gone."

Anil told Kwame about his interview with the Police Commissioner and his worry that Mona would be called in for questioning. But Kwame was not pessimistic. "It's a very good idea to analyse all that stuff," he said. "Probably the first time in history it's been done and I wouldn't be surprised if they discover that these herbal charms are mixed with bats' wings and snakes' insides and toads. That's what witch doctors do in my country and some of those old doses are supposed to be very effective. It will prove the real brotherhood of man – not this political United Nations' affectations, but the real cement that binds people everywhere!"

"That's all very well. But just suppose there *is* a bit of poison somewhere, then who will believe that particular charm was not the one bought by Mona? It's only her word against theirs and you can be sure that nothing will tickle the old oaf of a Commissioner as much as having a real live Indian girl as a suspect. He will probably go around giving press interviews saying she's fresh out of a harem or some such rot." Anil was in a pensive mood. "Everything is going to pot these days," he concluded gloomily.

When Kwame laughed at his depression and asked, what for instance? he started to make a list. Mona was still insisting that she had killed her mother; Pepe had been summoned by his grandmother to her *hacienda* in the country and rumour had it that that irascible matriarch refused to let him return to town until the last vestige of scandalous talk had died down; Gloria had been crying her eyes out and was not to be seen in La Boutique these days (she was heard saying that she would probably end up in a nunnery); the dear old Commissioner was probably at this very moment glued to his TV set watching some old movie about India, Gunga Din or some such rubbish; and to crown it all, Ram Nath, that veritable Jeeves, had joined the motley crew. This evening at dinner, he had presented a serving dish full of curried prawns without having laid plates on the table – and when reprimanded by the Ambassador he had just stared at him with a dopey, glassy-eyed stare.

"The only person, in fact, to have survived the flood," said Kwame with a grin, "is old H.E. He looks positively bonny."

"You can say that again. The old man is ordering porcelain like crazy. Did you see him making ticks in various books?

They are all catalogues of fine porcelain. He is even talking of auctions at Christie's and Sotheby's. It's a horrible thing to say but he has certainly blossomed since he became a widower."

"Hey, that's an idea!" Kwame sat up from his usual lounging position and said in a lower tone, "Suppose *he* bumped off his wife – the old girl's death was pretty melodramatic wasn't it? That would get poor Mona off the hook?"

"Nothing doing, he is far too cautious and meek. He doesn't even want to hear about illegal activity let alone indulging in something as big as murder. Frankly, I don't think he's all there." Anil told him about the interview he had had with the Ambassador and how the old boy had pushed him on to Bhagwan.

"My reading of detective fiction tells me it's usually the meek and mild ones who are the guilty ones. What about getting Mona to safety in the YWCA?" Kwame chortled.

But Anil was not in the mood for jokes. He was remembering once more the business of the stain on the dagger, Savitri's apprehensions which had seemed irritating at the time, and his own poo-pooing of the whole thing. Had he made a very big mistake in not taking her seriously? For the first time, he told Kwame all about that episode and its sequel.

"Man, you're the one!" exclaimed Kwame. "That dagger may have been the weapon that killed the Count and you have been sitting on it all this time, quiet as a mouse." He really was amazed. "There could have been prints, or some clue."

"And what murderer would leave his prints around?"

They argued the case back and forth. Who could have got hold of the dagger except the Ambassador? No point in thinking of Mona or her mother or the servants being involved in murder. If some outsider had taken it from the house earlier, the gap on the wall would have been very noticeable. But why should the Ambassador want to kill anyone, especially the Count? He loved being a member of the upper crust, the elite set; going to parties, entertaining big-wigs at his home. Savitri's dinners had been famous. Could there have been some hidden reason perhaps? Something political? Or supposing H.E. thought that the Count was getting too fond of his daughter and wanted to prevent things from coming to a head – but why kill him?

"Oh, stop talking rot, Kwame. You're getting to be like that old Commissioner, looking for a crime of passion. And keep Mona out of it."

"Where is Mona, incidentally?"

"Surely you realized her Pa got her out of the room to keep her from talking to you? They've probably both gone to bed."

Kwame was most amused and had a hearty laugh. Looking at his watch, he saw how late it was, close to midnight. They had been talking and arguing for a couple of hours, getting nowhere. He yawned as he got up to go home. At the door, he turned to Anil who was looking very depressed and punched him on the shoulder. "Tomorrow is D-Day and Zero Hour for someone in Calcutta, so cheer up!"

"So we hope," was Anil's gloomy reply.

Balbir, in a primrose-coloured turban, was at the airport. Once more, he had come in connection with the weekly bag but this time he was not alone. The second secretary, a pleasant young man with a frivolous outlook on life, had come with him to receive his parents, who were arriving for a short holiday with their son. Several of the staff wives had offered to clean up his apartment in anticipation of the parental visit. The second secretary was a very untidy person and he had accepted the help gratefully. His girl friend, Graciella, had turned up early in the morning with an armful of flowers fresh from the market and proceeded to arrange bouquets in jugs, glasses and even empty jam jars.

While waiting for the plane, Balbir looked casually at one of the booths selling local handicrafts, including some embroidered shirts. An out-going flight was announced and, happening to look up at that moment, Balbir saw the line of passengers forming at the check-in gate. With a feeling of *déjà vu*, he looked at a girl with dark hair hanging below her shoulders, wearing a navy gabardine trouser-suit and carrying a shoulder bag. He thought he even smelled the heady perfume with which he was now familiar. He rushed off to find the Second Secretary who was wandering in another part of the lounge, not hearing the shouts of the saleswoman from the handicraft booth, which followed him.

"Sir," he panted, having caught up with the Second Secretary, "look at that girl." He pointed to her. "She is the one I told you about."

After realising the Counsellor's lack of interest, Balbir had gone to the Second Secretary and told him the whole involved story. He did not think the Ambassador could have meant the Second Secretary to be excluded from this confidence; after all he was a member of the foreign service. The Second Secretary had thought it was a lark that Mona's passport could be in the hands of people who interested the police. He had had a good laugh and said that chances were against such a coincidence. He had told Balbir not to bother about it. But now he looked at the girl being pointed out to him.

"That's funny," he said surprised. "She does remind me a bit of Mona. A lot more sophisticated, of course, but there is something about her face. Perhaps just a question of the general type."

Balbir stared at him and then the girl. So that was why it had seemed to him, when he first saw her, that she reminded him of someone. Out of the blue it struck him that it was not so unlikely, after all, that she might be making use of the lost passport. The Police Commissioner had hinted as much. Nobody had really believed him, but there was a possibility that he was right. He should be told immediately that the girl was leaving the country again.

Balbir could not return to the office until the plane he was waiting for had arrived and he had cleared the bag, and this would take time – so he ran to the line of phone booths in a corner of the lounge, to call someone at the office. The Police Commissioner could be informed by phone. But there was a firm grip on his arm just then, detaining him; a furious, voluble woman demanded he pay immediately for the shirt he had stolen or she would call the police this minute. For the first time Balbir Singh became aware that he was clutching a shirt in his hand. It was grey with blue birds embroidered all over it and much too large for his slim figure. He was embarrassed and alarmed because he did not have much money in his wallet and could not afford to pay for the shirt. He tried to explain the position while the woman became more infuriated but the Second Secretary, thoroughly amused by the incident, offered to lend him whatever was needed. Balbir found himself the owner of a shirt he did not like and could not wear.

Mona was mooning around with nothing to do. She had no classes today, Anil had gone off somewhere, her father was in the office and the day seemed to be the longest in the year. She walked around the garden thinking that the plants did not look as nice as they used to. Probably her mother had given instructions to the gardener. She supposed she would have to look out for him and talk to him. But what would she say? She loved flowers but had no idea what made them grow or flourish. Manure and stuff, she supposed. Some of the beds needed to be weeded, that much she could tell him to do. The trouble was, she thought with a sense of inadequacy, she did not really know much about anything. The servants never listened to her, she couldn't even add up. And just because she was shy and diffident, lots of people took advantage of her. All her friends were so much more worldly and sophisticated than she was. Well, she was nineteen years old and she could not suddenly become matronly and full of wisdom – but she was going to have a jolly good try! She could even start by going to college – it was not too late to get a proper education.

At the end of the garden, behind the main house, was a small wing where the servants lived. She walked past it on her way to the kitchen entrance. She heard Indian film music blaring loud. That Gulati, she thought, he could never play his music softly. As a present for the tenth anniversary of his service with them, her parents had given him a small cassette player. He had been wild with joy. "You are my father and mother," he had repeated over and over, touching her mother's feet, and ever since then Indian film music had floated out of his room, and sometimes out of the kitchen, always played at top volume. He had even pestered members of the Embassy staff to tape popular music for him from the records they owned and he managed to get BBC programmes in Hindi on his radio when others could not get these on their far more expensive radios.

Now Mona heard the high soprano voice of Lata Mangeshkar, the well-known playback singer for many Indian films, trilling away in a song of unrequited love. The cassette ended with a distinct click and Mona heard voices. Good heavens, she thought, Conchita is in Gulati's room. She wondered if she was expected to be responsible for the servants' morals – after all Gulati had a wife and children in Garhwal!

"And that's what is worrying me," Conchita was saying.

"You said you left it on the first nail," Gulati said, sounding very different from the way he did when he came for the day's orders.

"Yes, and in the morning, when I came rushing over to you, I was so upset I had to come here. Well, then it was on the other nail."

"What difference does it make which nail it was on? You got in, didn't you?"

"That's the whole point! I don't know if it makes a difference or not and I want you to tell me what it means."

"Well, I keep saying it makes no difference… I don't know what you are so upset about…"

"Oh Gulati, please listen. I'm so worried. I always keep that key on one nail and…"

"Look, if you were so upset how did you know which nail the key was on, that's what I want to know. Women are always making a fuss about small things."

"But Gulati, I know it was the other nail…"

"Oh my God!" shouted Gulati, sounding most unlike himself. "And I am the one who is always being called a fool! Stop it, woman! You begin to remind me of my wife and that's one person I don't want to be reminded of. No more talk of nails." Sounds of soft sobbing floated out, and Mona hurried away.

Goodness, she thought. How different people are when you see them as human beings and not as servants. She had no idea what all that talk was about. It sounded crazy, getting upset because of a nail. She should not have been eavesdropping at the servants' door – supposing one of them had seen her! Feeling all hot and bothered, she quickly ran across the patch of grass to the kitchen and went up to her room.

SIXTEEN

Things Go Wrong

It was late afternoon when the news flash came from Calcutta: a single woman travelling to Bangkok had been stopped in transit and subjected to a search. Nothing had been found on her person or in her baggage. She had been furious and demanded to get in touch with her consulate; she insisted on protesting this violation of personal liberty and wanted to leave the airport immediately. She had missed her connecting flight in any case and would have to make alternative arrangements.

The customs officials politely but firmly detained her and removed her suitcases for a more thorough search. Eventually they found a small packet of diamonds approximating in value to the amount they had been told to expect. Experts in the art of concealment were impressed at the skill with which the diamonds had been hidden, and coded messages were sent to the authorities responsible for giving the information that had led to the culmination of a successful hunt. It had been decided, higher up, to keep the discovery from the press and so no publicity was given to this sensational find. The girl was in custody and, in due course would have to face charges in a court of law. Her consulate had been informed of the affair and an official had come to see her. Though powerless to help in a case of contraband, he had said that a lawyer would be arranged to present her case in court and he asked for names of her family members so he could get in touch with them.

He found the girl unusually attractive and tried to impress on the customs officials that in all probability the diamonds had been planted in her baggage. She was not the type who smuggled jewels. The customs officers, however, merely told him that they had instructions from their superior officers. As for the girl, after her initial outburst, she remained silent. She told the consular officer in a casual manner that since she was an orphan nobody need be informed of her plight.

Despite strict orders against publicity of any kind, some inkling of the operation reached one young cub reporter who was at the airport on the off-chance of getting copy, and an evening paper in Calcutta carried a few lines on an inside page to the effect that diamonds had been found on a transit passenger. No details or names were given and few of the paper's readers even noticed the small item.

In San Felice, very few eyes saw the message when it arrived but those who did were satisfied. Kwame's boss sent for him and said, with a broad smile, "So your hunch paid off!" Kwame was jubilant. During the night he had tossed and turned in bed wondering if he had made an ass of himself by passing on the information and launching a hunt which would be useless. He returned to his cubby-hole of an office in high spirits. Sitting at his desk, he began to wonder about the girl – who was she and what would happen to her now? The poor thing was probably the lowest rung of the ladder, just a stooge in the whole works. The real criminals would not be touched, they seldom were.

The only ones we'll get will be the carriers whose names Gonzalez can supply, thought Kwame, and they will probably get off with fines or short imprisonments. The big shots will remain anonymous and continue to flourish. What sort of an individual was Gonzalez anyway, selling out on his gang to make himself rich? But he must be pretty well in with the group and have their trust if he could give such accurate information, correct to the smallest detail. Kwame certainly did not look forward to meeting Gonzalez in the near future to pay him off. He felt defiled, as if he had been rolling around in scum and needed a good scrub.

He began to pace up and down the limited space of his office. It had been good fun, even rather exciting, doing the research and following up on the leads which had come his way. He had liked that. Meeting Gonzalez had been a lark too and he had worked hard on his boss to convince him of the reliability of Gonzalez's information and seen that endeavour realized. But while paperwork was all very well, he did not like that crawling sensation down his spine; one which had been acquired with his first tangible brush with organized crime. It was frightening. Kwame knew he wanted no more of it but of course there was no question of giving up now – this was just the beginning and he was the only contact with Gonzalez, apart from Anil, of course. Nobody else had a hope in hell of getting anything out of Gonzalez.

Thinking of Gonzalez's transformation from servility to cold betrayal, he could not help wondering what would happen if any of Gonzalez's people or his bosses had the least suspicion of his perfidy. So much for his Taj Mahal, he thought, and so much for Anil and me. Then, becoming his cheerful self once again, he started to grin at the thought of how scared he had been feeling a moment ago. Better warn Anil – he had to be told of the haul in any case and they must both take the greatest precautions from now on. No more meetings in restaurants, they must have been mad to plan so openly. Anyone could have seen them and they had no idea who was on the Other Side. Gonzalez had taken a pretty big risk when he had emptied his Aladdin's Cave onto the table the other day! He'd better watch out for himself, thought Kwame grimly, and I certainly don't want to be found some moonless night with my throat cut, lying in a gutter!

Anil was at the Academy of Handicrafts with Mona on one of the outings she was slowly returning to. She had been wanting to take him there for some time and he was given a guided tour by some of her friends. It was a very interesting place that offered classes for the study of silver and jewellery work, glass-cutting, painting, ceramics and many other crafts. Anil was impressed by it and enjoyed the tour. He caught a glimpse of the creative life, the endless possibilities open to the imagination of one with a skilled hand. For a change he felt refreshed by this contact with other lives instead of being burdened with other people's problems, as he had been of late.

In front of the academy there was a park and Mona took him there to show him where young artists collected on Sunday mornings to display their paintings to the public. They sat on a bench in comfortable silence and rested their tired feet. A gardener went by with a rake, scooping up fallen leaves and piling them into a huge bag.

"I must do something about the garden at home, our roses are looking awful," Mona said idly, as she watched him. That reminded her of pricking her finger on Sheela's rosebush and that conversation about washing off blood. She told Anil about it.

"But you know," she concluded, "it can't have been meat – that would wash off easily enough. It's not as if the meat was raw, it was just rare." She noticed that Anil seemed abstracted and shook his arm. "Hey, you're not listening to me!"

"Yes, I heard you. Let's go home now. I'm expecting a call from Kwame soon."

Suddenly the mood of the day changed and Anil was no longer relaxed. He did not want to upset Mona.

"You two are very thick these days, what's going on?" she asked.

"Oh, nothing special. Kwame just wants to consult me about some work he has, that's all." He did not intend to involve Mona in anything unpleasant. They left the park, talking of other matters and arrived home to find Sheela in a small sitting room, sipping a cup of tea and talking earnestly with Lupita. They greeted her happily.

"Hello, you two," she said, looking distracted. "I hope you don't mind, Mona, but I ordered myself tea and I've been consulting Lupita about a maid."

"What's happened to Conchita?'

"She hasn't been around for the last couple of days and the house is in a real mess. I have no idea why she suddenly left. Not that she does much but she might at least have told me. And she can cook quite nicely when she feels like it. I hope she hasn't had an accident or anything like that. Really, I can't understand it at all."

"But, Sheela," Mona was surprised, "Conchita was here just the other day. I heard her voice in the servants' quarter when I was passing by. Gulati is sure to know what the matter is. Let's go ask him right away."

The girls found Gulati Singh in the kitchen, singing off key as he put the finishing touches on what he called a Garibaldi. It was a spectacular-looking dessert made of alternate layers of coloured jelly and corn-starch pudding. The mound was now ready and he was preparing to cover it with a cloud of spun sugar.

"Just a minute, Baby," he said, "I can't talk when I am doing this."

"Then how can you sing?" Sheela wanted to know. He ignored her and concluded his masterpiece. Wiping his hands on his dirty apron he said, "So you want to know the menu for dinner? I have made the tomato soup but I have to fry the croutons still, then there is a…" Mona stopped him quickly before he went into a complicated explanation of all courses.

"We don't want to know what's for dinner. Have you seen Conchita?"

"Not today," replied Gulati. "I have been busy all day making lemon pickle. The lemons are cheap now so I thought I would do it. I did not ask you, Baby, because you had gone to school and I did not want to delay buying the lemons. From day to day the prices are rising in the market and…"

"Gulati, have you seen Conchita?" Sheela said in a firm voice.

"She came over yesterday but she made a nuisance of herself and I told her to get out." Gulati smiled, seeming pleased with this masterly treatment of a silly female.

"She has not been to work for three days," continued Sheela. "Is she sick? If she doesn't want to work for us, why doesn't she say so? I can find another maid."

Gulati was disconcerted. Where could as excellent a maid as Conchita be found? She was a good girl. He begged Sheela not to dismiss her. He had taught her to make many tasty dishes, including Indian food which the Counsellor Sahib liked. He started to list all the special dishes he had taught Conchita but Sheela cut him short.

"If she is not back by tomorrow I will have to dismiss her," she stated.

"She is upset about the nail, that's all," said Gulati. "This very evening I will go and look for her at her sister's place. Rest assured she will be back to work tomorrow."

"What nail?" Sheela asked, as they returned to the drawing room. "If she can't think of a better excuse, she's mad. What could happen to a nail except for it to break and that shouldn't prevent her from working."

Mona burst out laughing. She laughed so much that she could not speak coherently and Sheela could make no sense of what she was saying. Something about a key, but where that came in she could not figure out. Anyway it did not matter. Gulati will bring Conchita back, she reflected with relief. And thank heavens, Mona is getting back to normal.

At an office over a second-hand bookshop, some men sat playing cards. The room was fuggy with smoke, and beer bottles and plates containing the unappetising remains of lunch stood on a table.

"What's the time?" asked a man in a pair of faded, patched blue jeans.

"Just after six. No news yet. Do you suppose anything could have gone wrong? We've never had to wait so long before for an OK signal."

"What can be wrong? Just a routine run, not even a stopover." The speaker picked up one card and discarded another.

"Still," said the man who was worried, "there's no reason for such a delay. I keep wondering what can be wrong." He took a fresh bottle of beer and opened it. Taking a swig from the bottle, he wiped his mouth with the back of his hand.

"If anything is wrong," said his companion, looking up from his cards briefly, "it's your pigeon. You worked the route, didn't you?"

"And if anything happens to little Dolly," said another player, "the Chief will have your gizzard." He looked at his neighbour and winked, "Isn't that right, Romano?"

Romano shrugged. He was concentrating on his hand, rearranging the cards swiftly. He set them down on the table and said "Gin."

"Why, you coyote! You've been winning every hand all afternoon. Must be having awful luck in love." They all roared with laughter. Romano was no beauty and certainly not popular with the girls.

"Let's change to poker," the man in blue jeans decided.

They opened more beer, someone shuffled a pack of cards and someone else got out the chips. The telephone did not ring.

SEVENTEEN

The Ganges Floods

Bhagwan sat at his office desk, his head in his hand. He had no work but he could not make himself go home. And in the meanwhile, unaware of his mental crisis, Sheela seemed to be her usual carefree self. The house was in a mess without a maid and instead of putting it in order, Sheela had gaily gone out shopping yesterday and returned after he got back from office. She came in laden with boxes and asked him to admire some purchases she had made. It had left him speechless. Here he was in a state of constant suffering on her account and she was totally unaware of it!

He left home early in the morning and stayed in office as long as he could. Since the recent bereavement in the Embassy at least he had been spared parties, that necessary appendage to diplomatic life. As it was, he could barely get through his office work. The other day, Balbir had come to him in agitation and had told him about some woman at the airport. He had not been able to make sense of the words and had finally told Balbir to take the problem to the Second Secretary. Eventually the Second Secretary had come to him and explained in a cheery manner that all was well and that the police knew about the woman at the airport, whatever there was to know. He had not bothered to ask. Anyway, that was that. None of it concerned him.

His one concern was that tomorrow was the end of the week; the last day before his world crumbled around him, one way or another. No, that was not correct: he had no choice in the matter, his decision had been made long ago and therefore his last day was predetermined. In his state of perpetual worry, he wondered if it might not be worth his while to hint to the Ambassador that some kind of blackmailer was at large and see his reaction. Finally, he decided to go to the Embassy. It would delay his return home and he could check with Ram Nath about the mail. The office mail for the Ambassador had consisted of circulars and some thick envelopes with foreign stamps. Bhagwan had not been interested enough to bother finding what they were. Books, probably.

At the Embassy, Ram Nath said there had been no letters that day and he showed Bhagwan into the drawing room. On the coffee table, always so immaculately arranged in Savitri's time and brightened with a bowl of flowers and various decorative pieces, there was now a pile of books. A lined pad with a ballpoint pen was also lying on the table. Bhagwan looked at it and saw, with surprise, what appeared to be an odd list of purchases. The heading read "Herend Hungary Hand-painted Porcelain" and under it was scribbled "1 creamer, 1 sugar basin, 1 teapot." Then a blank line, and next, "meat plates, 8 or 12?"

Anil entered just then and saw Bhagwan looking at the list. "Did you know that H.E. has gone round the bend?" he asked. "Every day he seems to find a new catalogue of porcelain and makes copious lists. The latest is from Hungary – a firm established in 1839 and known for hand-painted dinner services and so forth. Very, very expensive. He can't decide between Bouquet de Fruits and Fleurs des Inde! He is sure to ask you for advice when he comes in. If he really buys all the things he's listed you will have to start looking for a new residence, this place is getting too small even for the catalogues!" Anil laughed but Bhagwan made no comment.

"What's up?" Anil asked. "You look awful – coming down with a bug?"

"I'm all right," Bhagwan answered curtly.

"Can I come and see you some time?" Anil persisted. "I have to talk to you about some things." He wanted to tell him that he was rethinking the significance of those daggers but there was no point in speaking about it now. For one thing, Bhagwan looked like death warmed up and for another, the old boy would be bouncing in any minute with more catalogues.

"My dear Bhagwan." The Ambassador entered as if on cue, predictable down to the open catalogue in his hand. "Good of you to drop in. Stay and have a drink. I have been looking at a most exciting collection of Nymphenburg china. Most exciting. I'd like you to glance at it and advise me."

Bhagwan stared at him. The man must be mad. And he had come to unburden himself and seek his guidance! Guidance, my foot! Old H.E. needed to be restrained before he really went around the bend. He made his excuses – Sheela was waiting for him at home and so on – and fled.

The charms from the village market, delayed by a week, had been collected at last. The task had been difficult because the old women had not been very cooperative. They had been amused when asked for a sample of everything they had to sell and had asked the policeman what his special need was. If they knew his problem, they would prepare a special mixture. He pointed to various piles of ingredients and inquired what they were and what they were used for. It turned out that some were herbal and others were made of animal matter. Some were a mixture of both. He had been horrified to learn that these so-called medicines contained choice rareties such as green flies, wild birds and ground snakes, among other unappetising ingredients.

The old women kept staring at him in a way he found most uncomfortable and presently he began to be afraid of their darting glances. He was not a superstitious man but he had the distinct impression that a spell was being cast on him. He had no idea what sort of a mixture Mona had bought and when one of the crones asked him if he needed an ointment, a potion or a charm to be worn next to the skin, he panicked and asked for a little of everything. He finally went off with a carload of odd-looking and strange-smelling substances, the cackling laughter of the old crones ringing in his ears.

The reports from the laboratory now lay on the desk of the Commissioner. He had not really expected to find any poison in the charms. That would have been too simple. And, after all, these were ancient recipes handed down from mother to daughter for generations. He knew plenty of educated people who went for regular 'cleansings' to these old hags. He wondered if people realized that they were eating ground bats and snakes, to say nothing of that big green fly his assistant had been told about! What fools human beings were. Well, that was that. There was no case against the little Indian and he was glad of it. He would naturally have done his duty if he had found anything suspicious, any vestige of poison in the samples analysed, but they were all quite harmless. Personally, he doubted that they had any power to cure disease let alone work magic. It was all in the mind, anyway. If you had to go in stealth to an old hag and buy a bit of evil-smelling stuff, you convinced yourself it would do the trick.

I must inform the young man of the results, he thought, and asked to be connected with Anil. Now that this red herring had been eliminated, he could return wholeheartedly to the murder puzzle and redouble his efforts. More than a month since Jorge had been killed and they were still in the dark. He called in his assistant and barked out some orders.

Now we'll see, he said to himself.

The swarthy man was having a shower when the phone in his bedroom began to ring. He finally emerged, a towel around his dripping body, to answer its prolonged and urgent summons.

"Yes?"

"The Ganges has flooded."

"When?" His heart lurched.

"This afternoon."

"All right." He put down the phone. He was still wet from the shower but did not seem to be aware of it. This was the first time, the very first time, any operation of this importance had gone bust. And what an operation – all those diamonds, the string of carefully cultivated contacts. My God. And little Dolly. He could hardly believe it. What could have gone wrong? There was no question of informers: every one of his workers was handpicked and loyal. He was a logical man and, casting aside the emotion natural to the moment, he went step by step through the whole exercise. No precaution had been overlooked, nothing had been done that had not been repeated hundreds of times before. Years of successful manoeuvres lay behind this operation. So who had alerted Calcutta?

Without previous information they would not have dreamed of stopping Dolly, a first-class passenger and a smashing looker. Poor Dolly, she was in for a bad time but she knew her way around and she would not break. He had excellent contacts in Calcutta but it was folly to think of helping her at this stage. He could not endanger the set-up because of his feelings for Dolly – an adorable girl, but there would be others. Time to get dressed and find out all the details. Every care must be taken to protect the syndicate, and the next consignment must be re-routed or delayed.

He started to dress and chose a tie with a scarlet dragon on it. As he was tying the knot he cast his mind over everyone concerned with the Bangkok run to see which one could possibly have had a reason for turning traitor, or had had the opportunity to do so. He could not immediately pin anyone down but he was determined to do so. That person would be rooted out and he, personally, would see him finished and done with.

Conchita was discovered at her sister's place by Gulati Singh. He was furious with her.

"There is your señora worrying about you," he shouted, "and you are sitting here calmly eating *frijoles* as if nothing is the matter. You must go back tomorrow morning. I have given my word."

Conchita recoiled at his anger and her sister too, who had been a kitchen maid in Jorge's large establishment, was quite awed by Gulati's show of temper. Still, she felt she must defend her sister's behaviour.

"Conchita is not running away from her señora. She only came to me because she was afraid. She thinks her key was used and supposing there was a theft, who but Conchita would be blamed?"

"Why should she be afraid?" Gulati demanded. "Your sahib was killed and the police came to question you, didn't they? Did you run away? She has nothing to fear. Making a silly fuss about keys. Anyway, I shall see that no harm comes to her." He turned to face Conchita, who had returned to her supper of *frijoles* and *tortillas*.

"Is it for this that I spent so much time teaching you to cook? What did you know except eggs rancheros? I have taught you how to make a puffy omelette and a good brown stew and Indian food as well. And now you say you are afraid to stay in that house!"

He pulled Conchita up from the table and insisted on

marching her home immediately. He ignored her unfinished meal and her sister's protests. "Better for you to be in the house to get breakfast ready tomorrow," he declared, as he swaggered down the road, shoulders swaying. Conchita sniffled as she followed a pace or two behind.

Anil was having a nightmare. He was running as fast as he could but whichever direction he took seemed to be a dead end and a dagger kept pursuing him. A dagger stained with blood. When it was very close and about to thrust itself into him, the dagger changed into a large brass key and then, before Anil could take the key to open a locked door, the door opened by itself and there stood Gulati Singh, smiling happily, with a baguette in his hand. He beamed at Anil and said, 'I am going to make you French toast for breakfast!'

Anil awoke, his heart pounding, and sat up in bed, thoroughly confused. This is the end, he thought. I shall go bonkers if I stay in this place much longer.

During the evening, the Commissioner had spoken to him, putting to rest his fears for Mona. He had told her the result of the analyses of the charms and her radiant smile had been her only reply. The poor girl had had a very rough time but now that she was no longer under police suspicion, his responsibilities to her and her family were done with. There was no real need for him to hang around San Felice. His brief visit had expanded to well over a month as it was, and he had to leave now. Mona would learn to make a life for herself. In any case, the idea of the marriage proposed by Savitri had been absurd.

He decided to visit a travel agency and book his ticket in the morning. But just a minute – there was that last matter of Mona's passport. Gonzalez had said that he knew where it was and that was a matter that had to be cleared up. Kwame might not remember to do so. His main concern was with the smuggling. Where could the passport be? With the smugglers, certainly, otherwise Gonzalez could not know about it, but how had it got there? Surely Mona could not have had any connection with a person like Gonzalez or any of his group. He would see to this tomorrow first thing.

He looked at his watch and saw that the time was 2.15; the dead of night, and no time to be awake and worrying. He lay down and pulled the covers close. This time, he fell into a dreamless sleep.

EIGHTEEN

In Odd Company

"I have to see our mutual friend today!" Kwame said to Anil on the phone. "Want to come along?" Remembering that they still had unfinished business, Anil said that he would come and they fixed the time. The meeting this time was to be in the lobby of a large hotel patronized by tourists. It was Kwame's theory that with a crowd of people milling around they would pass unnoticed. So many people met briefly for a business talk in a hotel lobby that there could be no danger unless Gonzalez was followed. And in that case no precaution would be of any use. The lobby, when they got there, was indeed very big with many potted plants and easy chairs scattered around it. In one corner a man sat at a piano and played popular music but in the noise of the arrivals and departures he could hardly be heard. A large tour group had just arrived and heavily laden porters were bringing in expensive luggage while the tour leader was at the reception desk, looking frantic as he attempted to keep an eye on his wandering flock. The average age of the tourists seemed to be well above sixty, and Anil marvelled at the sight of all these people on what appeared to be a senior citizens' spree.

Kwame and Anil selected a spot a little away from the main door but easily visible from it, and they settled down to wait for Gonzalez. He was late and Kwame was apprehensive, looking at his watch from time to time as he wondered aloud what could have happened. Anil kept telling him to calm down but he, too, was anxious. Suppose Gonzalez had been found out and eliminated – or whatever was done to renegade crooks.

Just as they were becoming seriously concerned about the delay, they saw from their vantage point the familiar stout figure of Gonzalez come through the revolving door, half an hour late. He stood for a moment looking around the crowded lobby and then saw them. Coming over swiftly, once more his humble self, he apologised abjectly for having kept them waiting.

"There has been some confusion in our midst," he said. "That is why I could not be here on time. I am sorry for the delay, sir."

"Nothing wrong, I hope?" Anil asked blandly.

"No, sir, nothing of the sort," Gonzalez assured him. "At any rate not for me."

Kwame opened his briefcase and took out a heavy brown paper packet, scotch-taped and waxed all over with seals. "Here. This is for you. You can't open it here but I suggest you go to the men's room and check that it's correct." Gonzalez seemed upset at the thought that the contents needed to be checked, and demurred. He, too, was carrying a briefcase, a very expensive-looking one made of alligator skin. In fact, he was dressed today in a sober Brooks Brothers suit with the tip of his gold pen and pencil set showing over his jacket pocket. He looked quite the senior executive. He opened his briefcase and deposited the heavy packet in it, setting its combination lock as he put it on the sofa beside him.

"At present, you understand, sir," he said confidentially to Kwame, "things are not normal for us. But a shipment is due to be on its way very soon and I shall be in touch with you. The terms will be the same as before, if that is satisfactory." He started to get up.

"Just a minute. What about the passport of the Ambassador's daughter?"

"But I understood that H.E. was not interested in the matter," Gonzalez said, looking at Anil with great surprise. "So many times I begged you to arrange a meeting but he could not find time to see me!"

"Damn H.E.," said Anil. "I am interested and I'm going to get to the bottom of the mystery so you may as well tell me what you know."

"Sir, sir, a little kindness. You are a very impatient young man. As it happens I have the passport with me and I shall be very happy to give it to you. I ask for nothing in return. My pleasure."

"What? So you were the one who stole it?"

Gonzalez looked pained at the suggestion. His glance was full of dismay at the thought that Anil should think him capable of such a deed.

"I have done many things, I admit, but I have never been guilty of theft. No, the passport was stolen, as you say, by someone else and it was put to use briefly. Then I was able to lay my hands on it and here it is." He took the small red book out of an inner pocket and handed it to Anil.

It was Mona's all right. Anil checked it and wondered how he could return it without a great many explanations.

"How did you get it?" Anil wanted to know.

"That I cannot tell you. Don't ask me, sir. However, you have been so helpful to me that I will give you the name of the person responsible for getting hold of it." He drew out a pocket diary and with a flashy gold pen he wrote a name and address on one of the back pages. Tearing it out he gave it to Anil. "*Hasta luego!*" he said and left the lobby with a group of tourists heading for a sightseeing tour.

Anil looked thoughtfully at the name written on the piece of paper. This was most curious. Where did this chap fit into the scheme? He handed the paper to Kwame.

"Know him?" he asked.

"No. Who is he?"

"I don't really know who he is but I met him in a most unlikely place. Now what can the connection be? I'm getting more and more confused. I think I'll go over and see Bhagwan pretty soon. He owes me some sort of an explanation, and I wonder if I shouldn't tell him about the dagger."

Pepe was back in town. His sojourn in the country with his grandparents had done him a lot of good. He looked rested and sunburnt. His honey-coloured hair was becomingly streaked silver by the sun. He had rung his friends to let them know that he was back in civilization and he wanted to have a party at the Safari Club that evening. Several people had accepted the invitation – Gloria with relief that Pepe was no longer in quarantine as, by implication, she too was over her troubles; Francisca with resignation because she was fed up with Pepe and loathed the Safari Club. Anil had asked why Pepe had chosen that animal graveyard for a place to celebrate his return and said that he was going to report it to the Wildlife Association. But he accepted the invitation with pleasure and said he would bring Mona and Kwame along with him.

"Of course, Mona and Kwame must come. If everyone clicks, my dear, we'll go on later to a marvellous paella place I have found. It's my very own discovery. Not elegant, but the paella is cooked slowly on a wood fire for hours and is too, too divine. But I have invited a number of people and some may be party-poopers, so don't say a word about afters to anyone. We'll see how it goes."

Anil was diverted by this conversation. In the midst of murder and police threats, it was delightful to picture Pepe wandering the back alleys of San Felice in search of a good paella. He promised, laughing, not to breathe a word to a soul.

Now that his departure was imminent he felt he should call on the Commissioner and take formal leave of him. The Commissioner was, of course, very busy but he spared time to see Anil, that afternoon. While talking to him, Anil remembered the name and address that Gonzalez had given him. He and Kwame had decided that the best solution to returning Mona's passport discreetly was to post it to the chancery – but they had not discussed what was to be done with the other information given by Gonzalez. It occurred to Anil only now that the best person to communicate it to was seated in front of him.

"I have reason to believe that a certain resident of San Felice got hold of Mona's passport. I can't tell you where I got the information but I can give you the person's name." He took the crumpled piece of paper out of his pocket and passed it to the Commissioner.

The Commissioner looked at it for a few minutes with the greatest interest. Aha, he thought, so the pattern begins to form. If this man took the passport, he was the one who gave it to the airport girl, that was quite clear. Hadn't he been at Jorge's party? Yes, he seemed to remember seeing him among the crowd in the garden that evening.... He looked up from the paper to see Anil regarding him with a curious look, and roused himself from his internal speculation. These matters did not concern the young man, bright as he was. But he would put the person concerned under surveillance through his plain clothes police right away, and he was sure there would be an interesting sequel.

"Thank you," he told Anil. "So you are returning to your wonderful country. Could I make a small request?"

Anil assured him that it would be a pleasure to do anything he could for the Commissioner.

"I long to own a sari," said the Commissioner, with a dreamy look in his eyes. "A really beautiful one with gold and silver and perhaps some elephants or peacocks all over it, like the one your *novia* was wearing that day of the reception at the Embassy."

Anil was speechless. Now I've heard everything, he thought. I *must* be bonkers. Why should the old man have a craving for a sari? But perhaps he had a girlfriend for whom he wanted it.

"I have always felt," the Commissioner continued, "that the height of elegance would be to use a really beautiful sari as a tablecloth. I have long dreamed of it. Do you think you could send me one? You see, the first function of a sari is to adorn a lovely lady, but after that it is the ideal setting for a formal dinner – the crystal, the silver, the choice wines, the gourmet cuisine – and all set off by an exquisite table covering of brocade!" He was so carried away that he did not notice that Anil was gaping at him. "Yes, silver or gold brocade and perhaps elephants or a design with your national bird, the beautiful peacock! I will be the envy of all San Felice."

I must leave before I totally lose it, thought Anil, and with the promise to send the most magnificent sari he could find immediately upon his return to India, he managed to escape from police headquarters.

The Ambassador was reading his bag mail. Before him was an official letter and he inspected it with care. In the impersonal jargon of governments it was brought to his notice that during the Republic Day reception held in San Felice, which had been attended by a large delegation from India, he had been heard to make certain remarks of a frivolous nature unbecoming his position as a senior representative of his country abroad. In short, it had been reported that he had suggested that national day parties were a waste of time. This matter had gone to the highest level and caused grave concern and would he kindly send his explanation at his earliest convenience.

Having read the letter, the Ambassador put it aside with his usual impassive look and went on to the other mail awaiting his attention. Finally, at the bottom of the pile, he came to an airmail envelope which was marked 'personal' and had not been opened by his private secretary. He opened it with a Toledo paper knife in the shape of a dagger and as he read the contents, a pleased smile spread over his face.

He sent for his secretary and dictated two telegrams. Noting a look of consternation on the secretary's face he felt some explanation was necessary – but then again, why bother?

"That will be all, Rustomjee," he said. "I need not remind you that these matters are to remain top secret until further notice."

He pushed all the letters neatly to one side of his desk and picked up his latest catalogue. It was from Vienna and he spent the next hour very happily thinking of Augarten.

NINETEEN

Baring Hearts

Anil awoke late in the morning, feeling rested. Pepe's celebration had been a huge success, first with the Safari Club full of his numerous friends and then, after the departure of the party-poopers, at the little restaurant where the paella had been every bit as good as he had claimed. There had been laughter and songs and even Mona, who had had to be persuaded to go to such a large party, had seemed relaxed and normal. She held no grudge against Pepe for telling on her to the police.

The grim shadows of murder and the underworld of crime had receded. Now, at long last, he thought, as he got out of bed he could finally see about a reservation for his trip back – he simply had not had time to do it so far. There was nothing more for him to do here and of course no question of his hanging about because of Mona. Fond as he was of her, there was no question of marriage. As for marriage, his mother was all for it, but she favoured an alliance with an Indian lady doctor in the States. According to a matrimonial advertisement which had appealed to his mother, this young lady had a green card, an apartment in Queens and did not consider caste a bar to marriage. Anil had laughingly promised his mother to meet the lady doctor before he returned home. But of course he had no intention of doing so!

As he went to have a shower, some partly obscured thought kept bothering him. There was something more he had to do but what it was, he couldn't imagine. With his second cup of coffee at the breakfast table, it came to him that he had to see Bhagwan. He had tried to see him once before but Conchita, with curlers in her hair and a sullen look on her face, had opened the door and said no one was home. The best thing to do would be to go over to the Chancery now.

In the hall of the Chancery, Anil was greeted as an old friend by the receptionist. He was shown into the Counsellor's room, where Bhagwan was standing by the window looking out at the busy morning traffic. With slow, ponderous movements, looking more like a brontosaurus than ever, he moved towards his desk and asked Anil to sit down. Anil was appalled to see the man looking so haggard. Though he hated to bother him, he was soon leaving the country and wanted to clear up a few things. It was imperative to discuss the matter of Mona's passport, for example. As Bhagwan remained glumly silent after his initial greeting, Anil decided to plunge into business right away.

"Look, Bhagwan," he began, "I met a man at dinner at your house one evening. What do you know about him?" He gave him the name.

"What makes you ask? What right have you to ask me such a thing?" Bhagwan's face was paler than before, the dark patches under his eyes more pronounced and his eyes stared ferociously at Anil.

"Listen, old man," Anil said, "I know you aren't feeling too good these days but..." he could not continue.

"What makes you think I'm not well? I'm fed up with you. You have been snooping around ever since you came here. Asking questions and being the little detective and helper of the Police Commissioner. But I won't stand for it. Get out of my room before I throw you out!"

"I'll certainly get out," Anil said, standing up. "But first I want you to tell me something. It concerns a passport..."

"What?" Bhagwan roared out the word. "What do you know about the passport? And who told you? If you think that you too can blackmail me, you are mistaken."

Anil was seriously alarmed. What had come over Bhagwan? He was certainly a different man from the correct but dull Counsellor Anil had met when he arrived in San Felice. All Anil had done was want to discuss the question of Mona's passport being taken by an acquaintance, if not friend, of Bhagwan's and the peculiar manner of its return via a smuggler. He felt that someone in the Embassy should be informed of this in confidence, and whom else could he go to but Bhagwan? But instead of a friendly chat he seemed to have provoked an avalanche! He was wondering if he should escape before he was crushed by it when the door opened and a head swathed in a cerise turban looked in.

Smiling broadly, Balbir entered. "Good news at last, sir, only this morning I have received Miss Mona's passport through the post."

"Get out!" shouted the Counsellor. Then, controlling himself with an effort, he told Balbir that he was busy and the matter could be dealt with by the Second Secretary. The door closed behind the surprised Balbir. Bhagwan stood up and looked wearily at Anil.

"So it is Mona's passport you came to see me about?"

"Naturally, what other passport?"

"I thought you meant the other one. Don't pretend you don't know what I'm talking about. You even seem to know about that bounder," sneered Bhagwan. The phone rang and after a moment Bhagwan picked up the receiver. A strange, blank look spread over his face as he listened, grunting once or twice in some sort of reply. Finally with a curt, "Yes, he can come to see me in an hour's time," he disconnected and glared at Anil. "So, you damned snoop, you have been very busy. Now tell me what you have told the Commissioner."

"The Commissioner?" asked Anil bewildered. "I haven't told him a thing except give him a name – the name I asked you about. I'm much more interested in the dagger." He was getting very angry with Bhagwan.

"Don't lie. That call was from the police office and the Commissioner as good as said that you had spilled the beans. He wants to come and see me."

"For God's sake, Bhagwan, what's come over you? I know nothing about spilling beans and bounders but I'm leaving town and I want you to know what Aunty said about the dagger..."

"So that's how you know," Bhagwan broke in. "I wondered how you had guessed, but if she told you... she was suspicious from the beginning, you know. She saw me looking at the daggers the day I was in the study to see H.E. about the delegation. The way she looked at me afterwards I realized that she suspected something and I knew I'd have to deal with it. But I hesitated – can you understand that? I didn't really want to harm the old girl. But what could I do? And when she made that remark about Sheela and passionfruit – she was always asking me to keep Sheela away from temptation. Anyway what could I do if she knew too much. About Sheela as well as the dagger, you see. I was done for. You do see my point don't you?"

"What are you talking about, Bhagwan?"

"I had to kill her there and then. She would have talked. More people would have got suspicious. Fortunately I had my sleeping pills with me. I've been carrying them around. I put a lot in the coffee I gave her." He stopped and rubbed his eyes. "That's how she died. I didn't know she had a dicky heart. I did feel bad for Mona, but what could I do – it was either Savitri or me. I tried to think of some way to tell Mona that she had not poisoned her mother but it was no good. I couldn't do it."

Horrified, Anil sprang from his chair and stared with

repugnance at Bhagwan. He could not believe his ears. He could only gasp, "Why, Bhagwan, why?"

"I've just told you. She knew all about me. You even said she had told you. No point keeping anything from you now if you already knew it, is there?" Bhagwan sat back in his chair and continued in a calm voice, as if he were giving dictation to Nair. No inflection, no emotion, simply a flow of unbelievable words.

"That night at Jorge's party, Sheela danced and danced with that damned Count. I'd had my suspicions before but that was when I was absolutely sure that she was going to bed with him. I made my plans before we went home. Sheela fell asleep in a moment, she always does. I went to the kitchen and took the key to the Embassy back door. Conchita keeps it in the kitchen. I walked over and got into the study." He smiled at Anil. "It was the Moroccan dagger, did Savitri tell you? That was the sharpest of the lot. I got to the Count's place – everyone had left. The servants must have been in the kitchen. The doors were open and I found him alone. The fool came to embrace me and I stabbed him. I don't think he knew what had happened. I didn't, until I had to pull the dagger out. If someone had come in I would not have tried to escape. But no one came and I went back. I washed the dagger and put it back. I remembered to wash the sleeve of my dinner jacket. God, there was a lot of blood. But I arranged everything before I went to bed. Nobody knew a thing. But somehow Savitri suspected and she told you."

Anil stood in a trance. This was a nightmare. It couldn't be true. He found his voice at last and asked, "What made you do it? If you thought Sheela was unfaithful why not divorce her? Why kill anyone?"

Bhagwan shook his head. He looked at Anil as if the latter came from another planet, unable to comprehend the mores of earth. He saw again a half-lit room and the nude figure of a girl – was it Didi or was it Sheela? He shook his head to get away from the painful memory. "She is my wife," he said. "I have to protect her. And as for that Count..." The mention of Jorge enraged him again and he let loose a stream of choice expletives in Urdu.

"It was not only because of Sheela... I hated him! Hated him for his superior ways, his degrading talk about my country. He used to go on and on about the poverty in India in that uncaring, casual way – 'I can't bear to see people suffer... I can never visit India because of the poverty... you Indians can never achieve western standards...' What standard, the starvation of the spirit? The need to dominate by every means, political, economic, with bigger and better weapons? He got on my nerves. A thousand times I had killed him in my thoughts! It was a relief to actually do the deed."

The telephone on the desk started to ring. Bhagwan ignored it. He was slumped in his chair, utterly exhausted, and Anil, staring at him with dazed horror, was unable to move either. It rang and rang and finally stopped.

"I would never have told this to anyone. Nobody had thought of me," he said after a long pause. "Now I shall have to tell the police as well. In a way it has been a relief to have told you – you are a good listener. Strange, I rather liked you from the first." He looked up at Anil. "Don't look at me with such loathing – you don't know what I have lived through. They say we make our own hell. Well, I know all about it. At any rate I never gave the passport to the blackmailing swine – that's something I could never have done. Of course you know all about the blackmail, don't you?" He rose wearily from his chair. "I'm really very tired. It's so long since I slept and those pills don't help any more. I'm going home now to sleep. You believe me, don't you?" As Anil did not answer, he walked to the door. Before opening it he turned around and looked at Anil with a sort of grimace. Then he went out closing the door gently behind him.

Anil felt paralysed. He was numb with horror, repugnance, disbelief, even compassion. What did he really feel – or could he feel anything at all? Bhagwan must be unbalanced, he needed medical attention. Should he call out to someone or phone for a doctor? But his legs were heavy and he could not utter a sound. I mustn't panic, he told himself. I'm in a state of shock. He began to take deep breaths, but his whirling senses would not steady themselves. How could Bhagwan be responsible for two deaths? Had he heard right or was he still hungover from last night? But even as he thought this, he knew that every terrible word spoken by Bhagwan was true.

The numbness was beginning to wear off a little and he went over the conversation. He would like to think that Bhagwan, in a state of mental strain, had had a brainstorm and crossed from reality to delusion, but all the facts seemed to fit together so he must have been speaking the truth when he confessed to two killings. And why had he gone off leaving Anil with this grim knowledge? Good God, in his state of mind he was mad enough to bump off someone else! What had he said before leaving – something about the police surely? No, he had said he had to get home to sleep, that he was tired... Sheela! She was probably all alone at home. Someone must warn her immediately. Strength flowed suddenly into his limbs and he jumped up and grabbed the phone. He dialled the Narains' number but got a busy signal. That meant Sheela was probably at home, unless the slovenly maid was using the phone. But he couldn't wait to find out, he could take no risks.

He left the room and ran down the stairs. Various people stared at him and the elderly receptionist shook her head and smiled at the impetuosity of youth. Around the corner from the chancery there was a taxi stand and Anil was fortunate to find a few cars in the rank. He got into the first one and gave the address to the driver, telling him to hurry. The mid-morning traffic was heavy and it seemed to Anil that the cab was crawling. Every time he asked the driver in a mixture of elementary Spanish and pantomime to go faster, the man shrugged his shoulders and pointed to the line of cars ahead of them. At each crossroad, the traffic lights seemed to change to red just as they approached. Anil was in a nervous condition, sitting on the edge of the seat, mopping his face every few seconds with a large handkerchief. All his previous apathy had left him as he sat, tense with impatience, waiting to reach his destination. They had nearly reached the Narains' house when the cab driver started to slow down.

Ahead of them, the street was blocked by a crowd of people. A policeman was waving his arm and telling them to move on; some of the bystanders were being questioned. A telephone pole ahead was leaning forward dangerously, swaying a little like a drunk, half of it bent towards the ground. A car which had smashed directly into it was totally wrecked. The cab driver came to a stop. He looked around to Anil and said, his face grave, "A very serious accident. The driver must have been killed immediately."

Anil got out of the taxi and stood looking at the hideous remains of the wreckage. Then, very slowly, as in a bad dream, he pushed his way past the crowd towards what was left of Bhagwan. In the distance, the wailing of a siren could be heard.

TWENTY

Debts Paid in Full

Once more, tragedy enveloped the Indian Embassy. The handful of Indian residents of San Felice were becoming apprehensive over the persistence with which misfortune seemed to be dogging their footsteps. Who next? they wondered silently, and with fear. It was uncanny, the way in which two hale and hearty people had suddenly died within weeks of one another. Of course it was common knowledge now that the Ambassadress had had a bad heart, but who would have thought it? A more energetic woman would have been difficult to find. And the poor Counsellor, a young man, slow and cautious in all his ways. It was very strange that he had crashed into a telephone pole.

Well-wishers rallied around Sheela and everyone kept asking how the accident could have happened. Bhagwan had hardly been the type to tear down the roads at break-neck speed. He was cautious at all times and more so when behind the wheel of his car – in fact he drove at a snail's pace. Coming home from a party late at night, having had a few drinks, such an accident might possibly have occurred – though still, surely not where Bhagwan was concerned.

But there had been no question of drinks in the middle of the morning, in any case. Several people who had seen Bhagwan in office, including Balbir, had stated that he had behaved normally and Sheela had been very surprised to know that he had been on his way home at that hour. He never did that, she reported, and was usually the last to leave the office in any case. He had been perfectly well and she did not suppose for a moment that anything had upset him sufficiently to lose control of his car. He just was not that kind of person. The whole thing was curious in the extreme and people shook their heads and remarked that there was no use looking for any rational explanation. According to an Indian proverb when death beckons, one follows. After all, it is all written in one's stars, they murmured.

The Ambassador allowed a decent interval to pass after the sad event but then, as he was fond of saying, life had to go on. He called a meeting of his entire staff to his room and made the dramatic announcement – he was resigning from the foreign service!

Everyone stared at him in disbelief, except of course Rustomjee, his capable secretary, who was in the know. The Ambassador still had a few years to go before retirement and they were surprised to hear that he had given up such a prestigious job. Perhaps the death of his wife had grieved him too much, poor man, and he could not continue in the diplomatic world without her help. They started to ask questions but the Ambassador stood up and made a gesture for silence.

"Before I relinquish my office," he said, "I want to thank each and every one of you for all your help and loyalty. Without your cooperation I would not have been able to complete my mission in this beautiful and historic country." He went on to speak of the cordial relations that had always existed between New Delhi and San Felice, his hopes that the ties between the two countries, geographically so far apart but so close in aspirations for their people as well as in efforts for the maintenance of world peace, would be ever strengthened and that the future would see many joint ventures in economic and cultural fields. He paid a graceful tribute to the excellent work of the Bharatiya Samaj of San Felice in popularising the culture of ancient India.

In general, he made a fine speech of the kind Ambassadors are accustomed to making at official farewell functions given in their honour. He was very good at that sort of thing. His staff was so flabbergasted that every one sat in silence and it did not occur to a single person to wonder why a farewell speech was being delivered on this occasion.

Only one man was able to voice at least one of the many questions which were springing to the minds of the others.

"Who will be replacing you, sir, and when?" asked the Second Secretary.

"That lies in the lap of the gods," replied the Ambassador, genially. "But you, my dear boy, are likely to be *chargé d'affaires* for a considerable length of time. An excellent training for your future!"

He then collected his various catalogues and with a solemn "Jai Hind!" left his office to go home for lunch.

Sitting back in his moss-green Mercedes, being driven home to lunch, he saw himself ensconced in a little mews flat in London, surrounded by his precious porcelain, a few choice pieces of antique furniture and of course his much-loved daggers. Gulati Singh pensioned off and Ram Nath, the perfect butler, catering to his needs and fixing his TV dinners. At the prospect of such bliss, a smile of pure delight spread over his usually grave countenance.

Mona, on being told of her father's decision, was startled. Too much had happened and too quickly, and she was unable to assimilate this bolt from the blue. How could she not have been informed of this major decision before it was announced to all and sundry? All she knew was that her father had accepted a post in London with a big multinational company, in exactly what capacity she could not understand. However, he was anxious to leave San Felice as soon as possible.

"Start packing," he had said to Mona in an off-hand way. "As for me, I don't really care to take along anything except my clothes and my daggers."

And what about the linen, silver, kitchen utensils, books and knick-knacks, thought Mona in wonder. I suppose I am to distribute them to the first person passing down the road! She marvelled at the private world her father had retreated into and was glad that she had grown up in the past weeks so that she could cope with things.

If Papa is going to London, I can try for college entrance, she decided.

Giving the unexpected news of their imminent departure to Kwame when she met him in the afternoon, she said, "My father obviously hasn't given a thought about my future."

"Let's get married," he answered tongue in cheek. "I think I would quite like being married to a nitwit like you!"

Mona was indignant. "Nitwit, indeed!" she scowled at him "And what kind of proposal is that, if you please?" she inquired. "Anyway I am not going to get married for years, if ever. I have discovered how badly I need to be educated. I think I'll go to London with Papa and enter a university. It's not too late to go to college, is it?"

Since she was only 19, Kwame did not laugh at this question. He put on a serious face and answered "It's never too late."

They talked of various halls of learning and Kwame, who had read economics at LSE, gave Mona several useful suggestions.

Anil had been absent from this talk. Neither Mona nor Kwame had seen much of him recently because he had been with the Police Commissioner or alone in his room with the door closed.

"He is acting weird," Mona told Kwame. "After all, everyone is devastated by Bhagwan's ghastly accident, why is Anil behaving like this? He wasn't even a special friend of Bhagwan's, always referred to him as a brontosaurus, and here he is in deep mourning, hanging around his room all the time. I just can't make him out."

As it happened, Anil was in that very room at the moment. He was playing a game with matches. The problem was getting a caravan of camels and a herd of goats, coming from opposite directions, through a very narrow pass in the Hindu Kush. Only one beast at a time could go across the pass. Anil had never been able to solve this problem and now he was convinced that if only he could find a way he would also be able to escape from the nightmare world he had lived in since hearing Bhagwan's confession and his subsequent suicide. Did Bhagwan lose control of the car or was it a genuine accident? This was the thought going round and round his head and giving him no rest.

For some reason Bhagwan had taken him into his confidence and told him terrible, horrible things. To Anil, his reasons for the killings of Jorge and Aunty had been anything but valid but it was pretty certain that Bhagwan had murdered twice and in cold blood. He might have been mentally unhinged but his final recital to Anil that dreadful, unforgettable morning in the Chancery, had been lucid, frighteningly sober and logical. Bhagwan had been a brooding introvert, not specially interested in people and intolerant of many things. Instead of having it out with his wife or suing her for divorce, he had gone mad at the thought of her supposed infidelity and probably, Anil gloomily conjectured, had killed the wrong fellow. There was no reason to indicate that Sheela and Jorge had been particularly friendly, let alone anything more intimate. After all, a man may dance with a girl without thoughts of seduction. The idea that it had to mean more was nonsensical but so typical of poor old Bhagwan.

As for Bhagwan being infuriated with the Count's absurd views on India and poverty, Anil could sympathise to some extent. He too had been subjected to a great deal of ridiculous talk on India not only by the Commissioner, but by several people he had met casually at parties. Many of these had not had the vaguest notion of his country and had waxed eloquent on what they thought they knew of its insurmountable problems. He had been appalled by their ignorance and had talked seriously to some while he had laughed off the more foolish comments of others. But instead of arguing with Jorge when he talked a lot of rot about India, Bhagwan had allowed the poison of his hatred to accumulate in his mind until Jorge changed from a well-meaning ignoramus into a monster.

It is odd, thought Anil, as he moved a match back and forth, that Bhagwan got so furious with Jorge's babbling about poverty in India. Surely he could have told him that most Indians were used to doing without things, that they were not conditioned to wanting more and more of the material things of life like people of affluent countries did. That while they naturally wanted the good life for their children, they didn't make a deity of material progress. India was certainly poor, but also immeasurably rich. An argument along these lines would have been stimulating, taught Jorge something, and certainly kept him alive!

And what about Aunty? Bhagwan had jumped to the conclusion that she knew he had used the dagger and left a bloodstain on it. The poor woman had been jumpy after the murder but she had not the foggiest notion that Bhagwan was involved in Jorge's murder. Yet her slightly malicious remark about Sheela and the passionfruit juice had sealed her fate and led to her death.

Anil had checked with Conchita and Gulati and uncovered the mystery of the key and the nail. Gulati admitted giving the back door key to Conchita so that she could come and visit him in her free time. She was an untidy girl but had certain fixed habits. One was to keep this key on one nail and a shopping list on another. She had become alarmed when she saw the key hanging on the same nail as the list of groceries because she knew she had not put it there. Who could have taken it and returned it to the wrong nail? She realized that if a thief got into the Embassy she would be held responsible.

While thinking all this out, Anil's hand had been manipulating the matches automatically. Hardly aware of what he was doing, he noticed that the camels were leaping through the pass one at a time, leaving the way open for the herd of goats! He stared at the pass, very annoyed with himself. He had never before solved the problem and now that he had done so, he had no clue as to how it had come about! Anyway, it was a good omen.

He pushed aside the goats and camels and took a pad and pencil. He started to write out a list of items:

Bhagwan got it into his head, without any proof, that Sheela and Jorge were lovers.

So, instead of having it out with Sheela he decided to kill Jorge.

He took Conchita's key, entered the Embassy through the kitchen, removed the Moroccan dagger from the study and walked to Jorge's house.

He stabbed Jorge and got away unnoticed because the servants were in the kitchen and dead tired after all the work of the party.

He didn't clean the dagger properly and left some stains on his jacket which stupid Sheela believed were made by juice from the rare meat.

Savitri, nervous after the murder, imagined a bloodstain on the dagger and later made a catty remark about Sheela, of whom she disapproved, and passionfruit juice.

Bhagwan thought she knew what he had done, got jittery

and put his sleeping pills in Savitri's coffee to stop her talking about Sheela's supposed love affair and the dagger.

QED Bhagwan was definitely responsible for the murder of two people and, caught by nemesis, had confessed as much to Anil.

Anil read over the list and felt everything was correct. He was dead sure that the swarthy man who had pinched Mona's passport was obviously a smuggler but where did Bhagwan's reference to 'the other passport' fit in, and who was the 'bounder' he had mentioned that day in his office? Why was he being blackmailed? And by whom? Oh well, thought Anil. I can't solve all the puzzles. I'll let the Police Commissioner handle a few things!

He had worked it all out, with Bhagwan's help, but what could he do with this unspeakable knowledge? Whom could he share it with? Certainly not the Commissioner. Good heavens, he could just imagine the headlines here, the consternation in India. And, almost worse than anything else, he could picture the old Commissioner dining off the story (at his sari-covered dinner table) for years to come, embellishing it with fantasies from the film world and his own strangely acquired tit-bits about the Orient. No, it was not to be considered for a moment. Bhagwan was dead and gone before a higher justice. Poor old Jorge had surely not deserved such a death, particularly at the hands of one of his guests. Aunty – well, let's face it, if her heart was giving out she might have gone at any time. But if the truth came out, Mona would be miserable and all her guilty feelings would return. Was it worthwhile telling the truth? Better let it rest. He read through his list again and then tore it up into small pieces.

At last Anil was able to book his return to India and say his goodbyes to all who had befriended him in San Felice. The night before his departure, he asked Mona and Kwame to dine with him at a seafood restaurant where they had spent many happy evenings. But the carefree mood of earlier times was gone forever. They were all subdued, forcing themselves to behave naturally and ending up feeling a bit uncomfortable. "What an anticlimax," thought Anil. He longed to take them into his confidence. He was so burdened by unwanted knowledge, but in the long run he felt he must avoid further complications.

"What are you going to do now, Anil?" Mona asked, after one of the long pauses when nobody could think of what to say.

"Well, the minute I get off the plane in Bombay, I'm going on a search for a fabulous sari embroidered with peacocks and then I'm going to tell my ma that I'm not interested in lady doctors with green cards!" At their astonishment he told them, with suitable elaborations, of the Commissioner's secret yearning for a sari and his mother's hopes for his future. For the first time that evening they roared with spontaneous laughter and just as Mona showed signs of getting hysterical, Anil said, "Now that we are back to normal at last, I'd like to make a toast." They raised their glasses and waited. "We have had too many deaths in too short a time. Let's drink to life and to the heroic and peace-loving, wherever they may be!" They drank to it.

And that is how it came about that Anil left San Felice taking his secret with him. He dallied for a while in New York, and then returned to Bombay where he rejoined his father's firm and led a secure and comfortable life.

Kwame, on the other hand, left the United Nations after a year or so and, as a freelance international journalist, he often lived close to danger, moving from one newsworthy place to another in many parts of the world and touching base in his homeland, Nigeria, from time to time. Both he and Anil kept in touch with one another and also with Mona, so the friendship started in San Felice endured.

Mona managed to get entrance to college in England where a new world opened for her. She so enjoyed it that she went on to postgraduate studies and turned into a fine young woman, full of confidence. Her father, no longer an ambassador, had settled into the mews flat of his dreams along with his porcelain and precious daggers. Peculiar though he was, and continued to be, Mona was thankful that he had agreed to let her continue her education and become independent.

Sheela, on her way back to India, was held up at an airport due to a delayed plane connection. While there, she chatted with one of the other passengers waiting for the same plane, a man who was also on his way to India.

"Why are you going to India?" she asked, not really caring, and was taken by surprise at his reply.

"I go every other year because I love it," he said with enthusiasm. "I like the great variety – so many different kinds of food and languages, dance forms and music. I love Carnatic music. Then the changes in climate from Alpine to tropical! And the amazing contrast in thinking, from ancient philosophies and Gandhi on one side to superstition and intolerance on the other! It is all so stimulating! What I feel is, *vive la différence!*"

Sheela stared at him with astonishment and then began to laugh. Soon, their flight was called and they went off together. It is possible they were destined to meet and perhaps they are now living happily ever after!

The name on the crumpled piece of paper given by Anil to the Police Commissioner at their final meeting was crucial to the solving of an important file. It was worth far more than its weight in gold. The Commissioner had immediately recognized the name and rightly surmised that it belonged to a man seen at a number of elite parties. He had lost no time in ordering a twenty-four-hour vigil on his movements. That is how a top dog in the smuggling racket was nailed by the Commissioner's officials and in time he was arrested. The arrest inflicted considerable damage on diamond smuggling in the region, but it also caused consternation in San Felice's high society. People wondered how they had so easily accepted into their midst a virtually unknown person simply because he was a smooth talker and so well-off! The Commissioner was concerned only about smuggling – he knew nothing of blackmail and its connection with the arrested man. No one knew it all except Bhagwan and, with his death, the matter ended.

While the Commissioner was satisfied with the completion of this case, he well knew that it takes time for a whole picture to emerge and that the worst of the bad guys can rarely be brought to justice. However, he continues to be haunted by his failure to solve the enigma of Jorge's death. Often, when he entertains friends at dinner (elegantly served on a dining table spread with a gorgeous shot-silk sari decorated with golden peacocks) the talk comes around to sad events of the past and all the guests raise their glasses in a toast to the scintillating Count.

Acknowledgements

Thanks to my family for their encouragement and also to Shri Balbir Chand who enjoyed the story as he typed the final draft of the original manuscript.